THE KINDRED SOUL OF
NORA FAYE

THE KINDRED SOUL OF NORA FAYE

LAURA C. REDEN

The Kindred Soul of Nora Faye:

The Tethered Soul Series, Book 3

Copyright © 2021 by Laura C. Reden

Ebook: ISBN 978-1-954587-01-4

Paperback: ISBN 978-1-954587-14-4

Hardback: ISBN 978-1-954587-34-2

Dyslexic Edition: ISBN 978-1-954587-03-8

Edited by Paige Lawson

Cover designed by Laura C. Reden

Cover Images:

© Adobe Stock / alexlibris

© Adobe Stock / krstrbrt

© Adobe Stock / Kevin Carden

© Adobe Stock / Stephen

© Adobe Stock / donfiore

CONTENTS

THE KINDRED SOUL OF
NORA FAYE

CHAPTER 1

I was going to live forever. It could have been a gift, or maybe a curse. I didn't know. But it was my second chance at life, and I intended to make the best of it. I never expected it would have turned out the way it did. This is the story of how my first life *should* have gone; and maybe then, I never would have been a Tethered Soul.

Every inch of my skin was sun kissed. My spirit sailed into the summer air as my body grew heavier in the poolside lounge chair. Without opening my eyes, I reached for the sweet Mai Tai, bringing the straw to my lips. The drink washed down my throat and settled like ice in the bottom of my empty stomach. I rolled the straw between my teeth before drawing another sip. A soft moan escaped me, and my lips curved upward ever so slightly. This was living alright. If I could do this every so often, I would surely die a happy girl.

"Why do we wait for someone to get married to

celebrate like this?" Brooklyn asked from the lounge beside me.

"I don't know. We should do this all the time."

"Let's do that."

"Uh, huh."

"Promise? You're not going to get married and forget about me or turn old and grumpy . . ." Brooklyn asked.

"What? Who do you think I am?" I forced my eyes open to look at her. The sunlight ricocheted off her oil-slick skin, nearly blinding me. She was starting to burn.

"Well, you know. People who get married stop hanging out with their friends and stuff. They get boring when they slip into a rut."

I sat up and reached for the sunscreen. "I'm not going to be like that. We're going to do this all the time. That's a promise."

"Good," Brooklyn mumbled.

"Now, you should probably put more of this sunscreen on; you're turning pink." Brooklyn lifted her sunglasses and peeked at her torso, then shrugged, waving me off. I finished the rest of my Mai Tai, the straw slurping the fine drops of liquid between the ice.

"Another round." It wasn't a question. Neither she nor I wanted this feeling to fade. I couldn't imagine a better bachelorette party. I told Brooklyn I just wanted to relax, and she booked a weekend away at a winery. We had massages scheduled, manicures, pedicures, wine tasting, you name it. If it was under the umbrella of pampering, we were doing it. However, I would be hard-pressed to leave this lounge chair in my current state.

When the sun's rays became too hot against my skin, I rolled to my stomach, draping my arm over the lounge. My knuckles lay against the cool concrete in the shade of my chair. "Hey, Brooklyn?"

". . . Huh?"

"Why didn't you ever tell Easton that you were tethered?"

A stint of silence stretched between us for so long I thought she might have fallen asleep. "Because I don't tell anyone."

"But, you told me?" I pressed.

"Well, that's different. I *had* to tell you. And you're my best friend, so there's that."

"Huh. True," I murmured. "Wait, why, though?"

"Why what? I need the server. Have you seen her?" Brooklyn asked, sitting up.

"No, I'm face down. I have seen nothing but my shadow. Why did you *have* to tell me?" I pressed.

There was a loud sigh, and I could tell I was killing her buzz. "Excuse me? Hi, can we get more of these?" Ice rattled as Brooklyn shook her drink back and forth. "And, do you want anything else?"

"Fries! Can we get some fries? Or, oh, chicken tenders! With ranch dressing!" I blurted my order out in fragments, the only way my brain was processing.

"Good call. Two of those, please," Brooklyn said.

I stood unsteadily and lifted the back of my lounge chair to a seated position. I fixed my towel, dancing as my feet burned on the cement, and sat back down as quickly as possible. My eyes adjusted to the sunlight once again and settled on a lady swimming laps in the long rectangular pool before us. "I don't want to die again." The scattered thoughts escaped my lips.

"Honey, we get to live forever. Just as long as you remember the plan, that is," Brooklyn said. I nodded, though I was sure her eyes were closed, and she couldn't see me.

"I remember," I said, thinking back to the day of James's funeral. Brooklyn had sent Easton away to tell me of a dream she had. I was accustomed to her dreams. I had heard about them all the time, and after the first few came true, I hadn't questioned them again. I never wanted to move to the small town of Clover, but when Brooklyn woke with a dream that my future would be found at Norton University, I couldn't refuse. You can't change fate, she always said. And that was true until she formed the plan. A plan to get around fate. "I know you didn't tell Easton that you were Tethered, but you told him about your dream?" I asked, my recollection fuzzy. It was nearly a year ago, and I had a lot going on at the time, with my memory coming back to me in fragments that would shatter my reality. I adjusted finally, but it took time.

"Yeah, I told him about the dream. He couldn't care less." Brooklyn waived her hand through the air dismissively.

"Really? He didn't care?" My brows stitched, and I pried my eyes off the woman doing laps to look at Brooklyn. She was surely burnt now. The pink in her skin turned to red honeycombs across her legs.

"Either he knows you're going to die and doesn't care,

or he thinks I'm a quack," Brooklyn said. Eyes gazing down the bridge of her nose as she lowered her sunglasses.

"Huh?" My jaw fell open, the alcohol hindering its closure.

"Don't get me wrong . . . He loves you; he really does. I don't doubt that for a second. But, I don't think he knows the half of it."

"Really?" I asked.

"Yeah, I mean, he really hasn't lived that long."

"Oh. Yeah . . . I have a lot to learn, too, I guess," I said, the weight settling down on my shoulders. I was still new, only on my second life. I might as well have been an infant.

"Don't worry, I've got your back," Brooklyn said. And I knew it to be true; she'd never steered me wrong. She had been there for me through thick and thin, and her dreams had been a beacon of light for us both. It wasn't until I came to her crying after I had seen the plaque on the bridge–riddled with confusion and distrust–that she told me she too was a Tethered Soul, and that was the reason she'd been drawn to me in the first place. She said my energy was a little brighter than others, the depth somewhat twisted. Whatever that meant. I hadn't seen the things that she and Easton spoke of. Except for the fairy lights I had witnessed in the clearing the day he proposed. Apparently, it took time to open one's senses to the other intangibles and invisible fields of emotion and energy. It all seemed weird to me, but then again, so did having a former life.

Chicken tenders and greasy fries came from the heavens above, and I dug in as if I hadn't eaten in a week. It surely felt like it. I became famished the second the first fry graced my tongue. The Mai Tai in the pit of my stomach soaked into french fries and ranch dressing, making for the most joyous of gatherings. If I thought I was happy an hour ago, well, I'd be wrong because there was a new standard now, and it included fried food. "It doesn't get better than this," I said.

"Just wait, it will," Brooklyn said with a mischievous glow.

A broad smile spread across my face. "You're right! We have massages!" I shimmied my shoulders to the beat of my jaw chewing. Brooklyn giggled, and I looked over in time to see her tilt her head to the side and shrug. She was leading on to something else, something I didn't know about. I didn't pry. Surprises were best served shaken with a dash of shock.

We finished our lunch by the side of the pool, and by the time I finally stood, I nearly fell backward onto my lounge chair. Brooklyn laughed, and I grabbed onto her arm for support while we strolled back to our room. She could have been more supportive if she had stopped swaying herself. We stomped through the bushes every now and again as we veered off the path, and each time we would blame the other. When we finally approached the four villas at the end of the path, Brooklyn fumbled with the keycard, trying to unlock our door to no avail. "Hurry up. I have to pee," I whined.

"It won't open!" Brooklyn jiggled the door.

"It's upside down!" I took the card from her and slipped it in what I was sure to be the correct way, but it didn't open.

"Wait, what room are we?" Brooklyn asked while glancing at her watch.

"We're thirty-one." I looked up to the door, and the numbers flickered in and out of focus. "Does that say thirty-one? Or thirteen?" I asked.

Brooklyn laughed, checking a message on her watch before grabbing my arm and pulling me forward. "Come on, I think we're in the wrong section. Our villa is on the other side of the winery."

"No!"

"Yes!"

"I'm going to pee my pants!" I claimed.

"You should have done that in the pool, my friend. Now let's go. We can't be late!" We trudged on for what seemed like a small eternity through grape vines and red roses. When we approached, the villa marked thirty-one—for the second time—our door unlocked with ease. I ran straight for the bathroom.

"Surprise!" screamed from within the restroom. I jumped, startled by the group of girls packed like sardines behind the door.

"What! What are you guys doing here?" I said, my hips swaying from side to side as they took turns in giving me a hug. Audrey, Terra, Grace, and Kennedy had all flown in a week early to celebrate with me, and to say I was shocked was an understatement. And then there was Payton, who came even though she slept with my boyfriend on my birthday. It had been many apologies later, but despite the regret she expressed and the full year that had passed, I still didn't trust her. And that would never change. But somehow, through the death of James, and the friendship of Brooklyn, we all remained friends . . . of sorts.

I danced my way to the toilet while the girls filed out of the bathroom, closing the door behind them. "We wanted to surprise you!" They yelled.

"Did you know?"

"Yeah, were you surprised?"

I washed my hands under the cold water, the sunscreen turning the sink water milky. I looked at myself in the mirror, my eye liner pooling under my eyes. *Good god!* I had to pull myself together! Fast! I was happy my friends were here; it just wasn't the surprise I'd imagined. With this crowd, I would have to kiss my weekend of relaxation away. It was a shift in mindset that I wasn't prepared for and was struggling with as I stared at my reflection in the mirror. I wiped under my eyes, smearing the liner as I opened the door to several expecting eyes. "I had no idea! You guys totally got me!" I said.

The girls squealed in delight, and another round of hugs began. "We have twenty minutes until our massages, let's start heading that way," Brooklyn said, managing our time by her watch. Her eyes must be more in focus than mine, and I wondered if she had drunk as much as I did by the pool. Then, I suspected that she had taken me to the wrong villa on purpose. I narrowed my eyes at her, and she returned my gaze with a mischievous smile. Brooklyn was always full of surprises. Right when I thought I knew her, she always did something I found shocking.

"You guys have massages too?" I asked.

"Yeah! We're not missing out on any of the fun!"

"I'm getting a Swedish massage."

"I'm getting the hot stone one."

"I don't know what I'm getting; I just picked the one I couldn't pronounce," Grace said. We all laughed as we left the villa.

"That's our room," Kennedy said, pointing to the villa next door.

"Yeah, and that's Audrey's and mine," said Terra.

Brooklyn swung her arm around my shoulders. "Payton is rooming with us this weekend," she said. I forced a smile. Several conversations were happening simultaneously, and my focus bounced back and forth between them like a pinball machine, never landing long enough to grasp the entire topic at hand. After trying and failing, I defaulted to taking in the view of the gardens as we passed by. The chatter passing in one ear and out the other.

Audrey opened the door, and the girls filed in. The scent of lavender washed over my senses, and the sound of trickling water came from various corners of the spa. The air conditioning felt nice on my warm cheeks, and I knew then I'd be falling asleep the second I laid on that massage table.

"Oh, you got some sun!" Brooklyn said, pointing to me.

I turned to her, shocked to see how red she appeared under the artificial light. "Me? You should see you!" I said, laughing. Kennedy and Terra laughed, agreeing with Brooklyn that I was far more burnt than she. If it were true, I'd be in trouble. Brooklyn checked us all in while I perused around the spa boutique picking up tiny purple gems and opening jars of mud that smelled like green tea. And before we knew it, we were handed robes and sandals and shown to the changing rooms. I picked a locker with the number three on it for the best chance at me actually remembering where I had stashed my clothes. Fifty-three. It shouldn't be that hard.

"Oh my god, Becca! You are so burnt!" Terra said. I looked down to where my swimsuit had shifted lower on my hips, and a stark white band wrapped around my body like a belt. My eyes grew as I rushed to the full-length mirror.

"What the hell?" I gasped. "I'm fried!" I said in a squeaky tone. The girls nodded, laughing at me in agreement.

"You are going to blister! I hope you won't be peeling when you walk down the aisle. That would be a nightmare!" Terra finished tying her wavy brown hair into a messy bun and picked at my side strap, examining my burn. "What's? You have something . . ." she said.

"What?" I lifted my arm, trying to see what she had.

"You have . . . what is that? It looks like you have a pen mark on you." Terra licked her thumb and began rubbing the skin on my rib cage. I twisted in the mirror to see my unfinished tattoo. My face felt impossibly overheated, and I was thankful that she couldn't see my flush through the burn of my skin. "It's not coming off." Terra continued to press into my side.

"Stop," I whispered frantically. Quiet as to not alert the other girls.

"But you have . . ."

"Stop, it's a tattoo," I whispered.

"What?! You have a tattoo!" Terra blurted out, catching everyone's attention.

"Wait, *you* have a tattoo!"

"She has a tattoo?"

"What!?" It came from several directions in the locker room and seemed to echo off the walls. I brought my palm to my forehead as everyone except Brooklyn came to investigate.

"Where?" They asked as they all searched my body.

"What did you get?" They stared right past it.

I gave up. Lifting my arm to the ceiling in defeat, but their eyes continued to explore every part of my body. The anticipation churned my stomach as I waited for them to realize they were already looking at it.

"That's it. Right there," Terra pointed out. I sighed, cutting through the shock and ugly gasps.

"OK. I know. I didn't go to get a pen mark on my side. I went to get an infinity symbol. But the guy totally messed up!" I folded my arms across my chest.

"No!"

"He messed up?"

"What!"

"How?"

I searched their hungry eyes but ultimately couldn't give them what they wanted. The truth tumbled out. "Well, he messed up when I leaped out of his chair!" I couldn't help the embarrassed smile that split across my face. Terra laughed, and Kennedy covered her mouth with both hands to smother her hysterical giggle.

"Shut up!"

"You didn't!"

The hazing belted from all five girls. Brooklyn was the only one who had already known about my mishap in Sin City.

"Oh my god, Becca! Only you!" Payton slapped her knee, laughing at my shortcomings. I didn't blame her. I did it to myself. And one year later, it was quite funny.

"Yeah, it's a one-of-a-kind, alright," I agreed.

CHAPTER 2

The seven of us stepped into the spa waiting room. Grace and I filled up on cucumber water while the others talked about how hot they hoped their masseuse would be. One by one, we got picked off. And when an exceptionally attractive man called Terra's name, the rest of the girls moaned in jealous disappointment. I smirked behind my handful of complementary grapes; glad it wasn't me who'd been called. I was the second to last called by a petite woman with a soft voice, and what I would later come to find as firm hands. The massage was relentless, and despite what I had originally thought about falling asleep, the pain of it all kept me wide awake, sobering me muscle by muscle. By the end of my forty-five minutes, I felt beaten and battered. Just the way I liked it.

"Make sure you drink a lot of water to help flush the toxins out," my masseuse said, as I left her room.

"I will, thank you." I took the water and drank it down in a few large gulps. I made my way to the ladies' room and showered the oil out of my hair. I took my time opening the bottles in the shower and smelling each and every one. I may have gone overboard when I found a eucalyptus spray that turned the shower into an invigorating steam room. When I emerged, I felt like a brand new woman. Slightly tired from the sun and alcohol, but refreshed nonetheless. I ran into Grace by my locker. "How was it?" I asked.

"It was good," she asked, uncertain.

"You don't sound so sure of yourself," I said, pulling open my locker, surprised that I had found the right one.

"Well, like, they really get in there you know . . ."

I closed my locker door slowly, revealing Grace's brown bewildered eyes. Her strawberry blond hair slick with massage oil; it almost looked as dark as her freckles. "Got in . . . where?" I asked.

Grace's eyes jumped to Terra, who strolled in. "Oh my god. That was just what I needed! He was so hot!" Terra let out a loud sigh and pulled her robe off.

"I mean, like, they all massage your butt, right? That's normal?" Grace's eyebrows pinched together, and she nodded her head, trying to convince herself that she was being ridiculous. I didn't know what to tell her. I'd never felt uncomfortable during a massage, and frankly, I'd never thought about what was standardized either.

"Well. . .what kind of massage did you get?" I asked.

Grace shrugged and shook her head. Brooklyn and Payton walked in chatting, and the volume picked up, echoing off the bathroom walls. "Like his hands were so firm!" Terra continued to gush over her masseuse.

"You sure it was his hand?" Payton teased Terra.

"Wow! Hey now!" I said, looking between the two. Terra laughed and wagged her brows, causing us all to giggle. Kennedy and Audrey strode in next, never missing a beat and jumped in immediately to tease Terra. If I had to pick a wild one out of the group, it would be Terra. She was a Spanish spitfire with unruly hair. Out of all my friends back home, Terra was the one who liked to kick it up a notch. I thought she might even give Payton a run for her money, but the night was young, and only time would tell.

We took our time in the spa's bathroom. Everyone showered and took advantage of the luxury creams and complimentary hair products as I did. I went on and on about the eucalyptus spray, making sure everybody tried it. By the time we left the spa, we were pampered to the upper limits and almost ready for our next adventure. Which, to my knowledge, was wine tasting and dinner reservations. The only thing we had to do in preparation was get dressed and maybe put on a little bit of makeup, and we'd be tasting in no time.

Nearly two hours later, we emerged from our rooms. Everyone appeared to be the best versions of themselves, and voices clamored in the air about clothes pairings and eye shadow. Audrey, in particular, loved my heels, and we somehow had a full conversation about them and them alone on the way to the wine tasting room.

"Well, have you tried the moleskin?" Audrey asked, her hand wrapped around the crook of my arm.

"Moleskin?" My upper lip curled as we walked into a large tasting room. Wine-soaked barrels permeated the frigid air, and I took a deep breath in before letting out a shudder.

"Just try it. You'll thank me later," Audrey said, patting my arm before letting go. I looked back at her and nodded. I'd have to remember the stuff and try it. But somehow, I knew that coming off the bachelorette weekend high, I would never remember a second skin made of a rodent. I shrugged to myself in contemplation as I stepped up to the bar. I took out my ID and slid it to the bartender; it never got old.

"Which one are you going to start with?" Audrey asked.

I scanned over the list of tasters. "I think I'm going to do the reds. Oh, look, the port comes with a chocolate!" I said.

"Sold. I want that one. Think I could start with that one?" Audrey asked.

I laughed. "I think you have to go in order, but you could ask?"

Grace slinked up beside me while I waited for my pour. "I don't know what I like. What should I get?" she asked.

"Um, I don't know. Why don't you start with a light white wine?" I said. Grace nodded and pointed to the first white wine on the tasting menu. In the dim lighting, her hair looked void of red and she could easily pass as brunette. I smiled up at her timidness and watched as her brows furrowed with thought.

"Are you sure you want to marry this guy?" As soon as it slipped out of her mouth, the fear set in, and she tried to cover her misstep. "No! I mean, I don't mean are you sure, I mean, you're sure? Like how do you know you're sure? . . . When did you know you were sure?" Grace took a breath and stared at me with beady eyes waiting to assess the damage.

I giggled and took a sip of my first taster. Tart. The back of my jaw came to life. "You're fine! I know what you mean. He's the one. I just know it." I said, my cheeks warming.

Grace stared, her eyes unblinking. "But *how* do you know? I don't even know what wine I want to commit to tasting. How could you possibly know what man you want to spend the rest of your life with?" she asked, making a valid point. I could see how one might be perplexed over this very question. And I was so young. How was I to know what I wanted? But the answer was simple; I just knew.

Kennedy's brows rose and nodded as she joined the interaction making it two to one. "Yeah, how do you know?" she asked.

I sighed, my cheeks surely beet red, and that was before the embarrassment. Audrey and Terra turned around to make four pairs of eyes, staring and waiting for me to say something profound. I wasn't the first man on the moon, but I was the first out of my friends to get married, and that was pretty close. "Because I can't imagine my life without him. And I wouldn't want to," I said, skirting around all of our history.

It would have been easier to say that I'd died once, and my heart refused to let him go. My love for him was so strong that he literally breathed new life into me. It would have been easier to say that I never had a choice. That my heart picked his, or vice versa–I'm not sure–but whatever had happened was outside of my control. That it was fate, and it was bigger than him or me. But because saying all of that was not an option as I stood, twirling my glass with one sip left, I said this: "When you know, you know!"

To their dissatisfaction, each and every one of the four girls groaned in protest. Greedy, wanting more direction. As if I had somehow found the key to success and refused to share it with them. I swallowed my last taste, and my next pour came without asking. Dry. Fruity. Better than the last. It reminded me of my second life.

"But you've only known him for a year, how do you know?"

"Yeah, I've dated Landon for three years, and never once was I like, 'This is the man I want to marry!'"

I laughed, touching my glass to my nose and trying to hide behind its transparency. "That's because you didn't know!" I exclaimed.

"Exactly!"

"Exactly!" I agreed. "If you knew, it would be a different conversation, right? It would be more like, 'I never want to be apart from him. I love him now, and I'll love him till the end of time! And I can't wait to share my life with him,'" I said, noting a raised eyebrow from Brooklyn one wine barrel away.

"That's so sweet, Becca. I'm so happy for you," Grace said.

I smiled at her, and she leaned in for a quick hug. Her hand lingered on my back, rubbing away her worry. "Grace, you don't have to worry about it. You will know. And if you don't know, maybe he's not the right one," I said. She finished her pour of white and bared her bottom teeth, wincing. "You don't like it?" I asked.

"Oh, I love it!" Grace said, eager to please, but it was anything but the truth.

"No offense to you . . ." Terra started. I braced myself for the undoubtedly offensive comment about to spill from her lips. "I just don't think I could ever be sure that I wouldn't want a different man in my life. Like, how could you pick one, and only one? I don't think I could settle for just one," Terra said, eyes crossing in a downward gaze. Grace's lips pulled down as she looked away. Audrey's eyes grew large and fixated on my expression. "But like, no offense," Terra snapped out of her trance and waved her hand, erasing rude parts of her comment.

"It's OK. Marriage isn't for everyone. And if you feel like you're settling, I would highly recommend you don't marry! But for me, I wouldn't settle if I had anything less than Easton," I said. And the truth was, I wasn't offended by what she'd said. I knew that she just hadn't met the right person yet, and one day if she did, she would have a different perspective altogether. If she didn't, well, at least she wouldn't "settle," and that was fine too.

Terra must have felt bad for her comment because she spent the rest of the wine tasting trying to make it up to me with over-the-top compliments and gestures. I must have told her three separate times her comment didn't bother me, but when she wouldn't let it go, I told her we could call it even if she gave me her port chocolate. She gladly gave it up, and I savored the dark, bitter-sweet chocolate between sips of the syrupy port. By the time we had strolled to dinner, my heels were in my hands, and I padded barefoot down the pathway.

Dinner was a perfect mixture of laughter and delicious bread rolls. The wine helped keep my body warm in the air-conditioned restaurant as I picked at my plate of chicken and potatoes au gratin. We talked about the wedding briefly, going over the final dress fittings and place settings. I filled in Payton about how Brooklyn and I knew the rest of the girls from back home. Grace and I met in the third grade when I had to take her to the nurse's office after she scraped her knee on the asphalt. She cried the entire way there, and I remember it feeling like life or death in the moments it took to walk to the main office. She was friends with Kennedy, and I slipped into their small friend group seamlessly after that day. I met Brooklyn, Audrey, and Terra in high school. But when the conversation pivoted, and the girls wanted to know how I'd met Payton, the air shifted, and I was no longer warm.

"And you met Payton at Norton University?" Audrey asked.

"Yes, she was friends with a couple of the guys there, Nolan and James. And Nolan and I shared a class, so we started hanging out," I explained.

"Isn't Nolan the guy who cheated on you?" Audrey asked. Though it was an innocent comment, my stomach churned. My face flushed. They had no idea that Payton was the one who he'd cheated with.

"Um, yeah. But we weren't exclusive or anything, so . . ." I said, trying to diffuse the conversation.

"Still, what a dirtbag!" Audrey said of Nolan.

"And didn't he sleep with your friend or something?" Terra pressed.

Acrobats flipped in my stomach. The whole circus had shown. I stuttered. "Uh, uh, he . . ." My eyes jumped to Payton, and I wish they hadn't. Her head held high in a dismissive fashion. It only made me angry.

"Oh, and wasn't James the one who died?" Terra continued, digging the entire table into a hole we could not escape from.

My face drained, and somehow, I wished we were still talking about Payton and Nolan. I found I preferred anger to helplessness and sorrow, and I would rather dwell on how Nolan cheated on me than how James was denied a long and beautiful life that he very much deserved. I could not answer the questions as they came.

"Yes, James is the one who had the accident," Brooklyn said, as a matter of fact.

"Oh, shit! I'm so sorry, you guys. It's been a tough year, huh?" Terra said, looking from Brooklyn, Payton, and me.

Brooklyn squeezed my hand under the table, and my eyes dropped to my half-eaten chicken.

Payton nodded. "The worst," she said.

CHAPTER 3

$\mathcal{P}$ayton drowned her regret with another glass of wine. At least, I assumed it was regret. Perhaps she was just uncomfortable with the topic, or the point of view at which it was shared. I knew she had her reasons for sleeping with Nolan, and none of it was shared at the dinner table that night. Thank god. But it caused for an uncomfortable walk back to our villas. Payton and I couldn't be further from each other as she led the way, and I trailed in the back. I didn't know what to expect when Brooklyn, Payton, and I were alone in our villa for the night, and I didn't want to find out.

But when Payton unlocked the door and an exceptionally well-built firefighter was sitting at the dinette set, I knew I wouldn't have to deal with Payton for quite some time yet. His blond hair was a mess, and his stubble had been growing just long enough to give the illusion that he was a little rough around the edges. A bad boy, helping good people. He stood to his full height, making me feel small, and when all the girls pointed directly at me, I melted. My insides disintegrated, leaving me with not a bone to stand on. This guy was unbelievably attractive, and I didn't want to take my eyes off him. But the last thing I wanted was for him to notice me at all.

He strode towards me. My stomach lurched as he swooped me off my feet and placed me on a chair in the middle of the villa. Brooklyn started playing music, and Payton started pouring shots. The girls were hollering, and the bass bumping. All of it was happening so fast my head began to swim. And then his jacket was coming off. The screaming began as my friends turned into feral beasts. He peeled his jacket off his arms, exposing his shirtless, very tan abs and red suspenders as he swung the jacket overhead. He placed it around Kennedy's shoulders, and she screamed, jumping up and down as if her teen crush pop star had reached downstage and grazed her fingertips.

I sat motionless in the wrought-iron seat in the middle of the room. Hiding in plain sight. Brooklyn passed by and placed a tiara on my head, and Audrey draped a sash over me that read, "bachelorette." As if I wasn't already a target, now I had a red bullseye painted across my chest. I didn't want any of it. The stripper turned his attention back to me, placing his boot between my legs, resting on the edge of my seat. I spread my legs, not wanting the sole of his boot to touch my jeans. My back straightened as it pushed against the chair. I noticed some of the girls laughing at my expression, and I tried to loosen up, but my face was frozen in shock.

The firefighter's hips rolled to the beat of the music as

he slid one red suspender off his shoulder to hang waist side. And then another. Before I knew it, oil was being rubbed down his chest and onto his abs. My eyes were transfixed, and I was pretty sure I hadn't blinked since we arrived at the villa. Then, a collision of fear and excitement plowed through me. I swallowed hard, and when he turned to let the other girls help rub the oil in, I escaped from the hot seat.

The girls hooted and hollered, and I grabbed a shot on my way out of the villa. I threw it back before the door closed behind me. And I was thankful to hear that the commotion continued in my absence. I walked to a nearby row of grapevines and sat under a trellis near the parking lot. Taking a deep breath, I did what I knew was forbidden on a night like tonight. I called Easton.

"Hello?" Easton answered on the other line. My heart warmed at the sound of his voice.

"Hello," I said.

"Is everything OK?"

"Yeah," I said, small and meek.

"Beck, what's wrong?" Easton asked.

I sighed. "Nothing's wrong. I just wanted to hear your voice."

There was a pause on the line. "I miss you too. I'm just picking up my brother from the airport; he should be out any minute."

"Are you excited to see him?" I asked.

"Yeah, I think it will be nice. I haven't seen him since I moved to Clover. It's probably been over three years or so—"

"They got a stripper. . ." I blurted out, unable to hold it back any longer.

Easton laughed carelessly on the other end, and I didn't know if I should be relieved or offended. "I know. Brooklyn told me everything before you left. Is he as good-looking as she said he would be?" he asked, sounding genuine.

My face flushed as I walked my fingers around on the bench. "Seriously?" Sometimes I questioned if he had a jealous bone in his body. Not that I wanted that. I didn't. But I could have stood to hear a little worry in his tone.

"Well, I mean, I know he's not as ripped as I am, but she said he'd be good-looking." Easton laughed at himself, and I joined in. A commotion sounded on the other line, and then I heard a door slam shut. "Hey, man. Good to see you!"

"Hey, brother!"

"Beck, say hi to Tanner . . . She's on speaker," Easton said.

I smiled, though he couldn't see me. "Hi Tanner, I can't wait to see you," I said.

"Hey, neighbor!" Tanner said. It seemed like a lifetime ago, but I managed to hold on to a few memories of Tanner. From what I remembered, he wasn't half bad. Of course, Easton was my favorite.

"Well, listen, I don't want to keep you from all the fun–she has a stripper–"

"No way!"

I rolled my eyes, having the news spread like wildfire.

"Yeah. So go have a good time. Not too much fun,

though, you hear?" Easton said. And there it was, the bit of worry I'd been waiting for.

I laughed. "Alright," I said with a big, goofy smile. Someone caught my eye in the dark of the night, and when I turned, startled, I was glad to see it was Brooklyn approaching me.

"Now's your chance, Bec. Once you're married to this fool, there will be no turning back!" Tanner yelled in the background.

"OK, I'll go have some fun. I look forward to seeing you again, Tanner. Make yourself at home."

"You know I will!" he replied.

"I love you," Easton said.

Brooklyn sat down on the bench beside me. I smiled up at her and held up a finger. "I love you too. Bye."

"Bye."

Brooklyn put her arm around my shoulders. "Everything OK? I've been looking everywhere for you."

"Oh yeah, I just wanted to call Easton." I shook my phone.

"You know that's strictly against the rules, right?"

I chuckled, and Brooklyn's face cracked into a sympathetic smile. "I'm sorry, I'm terrible at this."

"Yes. You are. What's the problem? Is he not hot enough for you? Because I told them to send the hottest one," Brooklyn asked, half-joking, half-seriously confused.

"No, god no. He's . . . great. Um, he just makes me a little uncomfortable." I smiled apologetically.

Brooklyn laughed and shook her head. "Well, honey, I don't get you, but that's OK. You can't be worse than Grace.

She's back there cowering in the corner. I think she might have locked herself in the bathroom when I left." Brooklyn laughed.

I laughed and clutched my hand to my mouth. "Oh no! Poor Grace. We should go save her."

"Yes, you probably should. Come on; it won't be that bad. I promise." Brooklyn stood and pulled me to my feet. We began walking back to the villa, and this time, I was sure we were headed in the right direction. "Are you OK with the whole Nolan thing?" she asked.

"Oh my god! That was so awkward!" My eyes bulged as I grabbed hold of her arm and squeezed.

"They don't know it was Payton, huh?" she raised her eyebrows at me.

"Not a clue!" I said, exchanging a look of unease between us.

"What's Easton doing tonight?" she asked, changing the topic.

"He's picking up his brother, Tanner."

"Oh! Is he single?" Brooklyn wagged her eyebrows. I laughed and gave her a light shove. She giggled and took the crown off my head. "Don't worry. I've got this. Just have fun, OK?" Brooklyn flashed a mischievous smile.

We slipped into the room unnoticed. The stripper was down to a red thong, and his suspenders draped down the sides of his legs. His pelvis hadn't stopped thrusting and rolling since I'd left. And I was pretty sure the drinks hadn't stopped flowing, either. Brooklyn whooped and hollered, dancing up to Payton and placing the crown on her head. She didn't think a thing of it as she shimmied with her empty shot glass. Brooklyn said something into the stripper's ear, and he nodded. I had a feeling I was off the hook. I pulled the sash over my head and took a deep breath before joining the fun without a target on my back.

The party continued for another couple of hours or so. When I thought I couldn't possibly laugh any longer, I did. Terra fell off the bed at least three times, and Payton slow danced with the stripper. The other girls never stopped dancing as Grace and I cried with laughter. By the time the firefighter was dressed again and ready to go home, the party had clearly come to an end. The girls were beyond tired, and the music had died down to white noise. Shoulders were slumped, and mascara smudged as all the girls had outdone themselves. My cheeks hurt so bad; they would be sore tomorrow. I thanked the gentleman on his way out. I thanked each of my friends with hugs as they trickled out of the room and off to bed. And when the door finally closed, and all was quiet, I looked around to find Payton asleep at the foot of the bed. I looked to Brooklyn and shrugged.

"That wasn't too bad, right?" Brooklyn asked.

I shook my head. "I haven't laughed like that in a long time. I had a lot of fun. Thank you," I said, sincerely.

"Did you see him suck Terra's toes?" Brooklyn's eyes bulged.

"Oh! Oh my god! I just about died! It was the most disgusting thing I've ever seen!" I grabbed my stomach, still churning at the memory. We chuckled, recapping the night while we took off our makeup in the bathroom.

When we were done in the bathroom, Brooklyn curled

up in the bed that Payton lay across while I got the other bed to myself. I closed my heavy eyes and drifted off to sleep. But it wasn't long before I woke to sounds of vomiting from behind the closed bathroom door. I squinted my eyes and assessed my surroundings. Payton was gone, and Brooklyn was fast asleep, mouth agape and snoring as she often did after a night of heavy drinking.

I tiptoed into the restroom, holding a bottle of water. Payton's cheek lay across the toilet seat lid. "Oh, Payton . . . are you OK?" I asked. Clearly, she'd had better days.

"Nooo. I'erd too mush," Payton mumbled.

My head ached, too, but I was in no position to complain. "Try to drink some water," I said, holding out the bottle for her. She took it, taking slow sips as if she had fallen back asleep between each one. Her body convulsed, and I grabbed the water from her. Awful sounds escaped her throat like the exorcist had been trying to escape. She retched, vomiting into the toilet. I gathered her hair, holding it back while she emptied the entire contents of her stomach. When her episode had calmed, I fetched her a wet wash cloth and ice. She wiped her mouth and nose while I tied her hair back.

I sat down against the bathroom cabinets and rested my head on my knees. We sat in silence. Both probably drifting in and out of consciousness, until her voice brought me back sometime later.

"I'm surry," she slurred.

I lifted my head and looked about the bathroom. "Sorry?" I asked.

"I'm surry fer what I did." Payton's eyes had parted, and she stared at me through tiny watery slits of her lids.

I took a deep breath, already having known that this apology would come after the dinner conversation had dug up the past. "We talked about this already. I know you're sorry. It's OK." The truth was, it was more complicated than that. I couldn't control the standards that she held herself to, and we weren't very close friends when it happened. And if it hadn't happened the way it did, would I still have run into Easton's arms? I wasn't sure. I'd like to think so, but who's to say. Did that make sleeping with Nolan OK? No. It didn't. But it was hard to say I'd been damaged after I had come out on top.

"Iz not OK. I'm surry," Payton repeated.

I watched her for a moment while I tried to gather my thoughts. The truth was, it all seemed so insignificant after James had died. Somehow, it seemed like it was a choice that she and Nolan had made about how they wanted to live their lives. And as long as I did nothing that I was ashamed of, I was honestly OK with what had happened. I didn't feel like a victim because I lost nothing but a few nights' sleep. And actually, it felt like I had nothing to do with it in the first place. I couldn't understand where she and Nolan were coming from when they did it, but I didn't need to.

I said the only thing I could think of. "I forgive you." Payton closed her eyes, and a small lone tear crossed the bridge of her nose. It was true. I had forgiven her, but I wasn't one to forget as easily.

I opened the door, Brooklyn on my heels, holding my pillow. I tossed my bag in the entryway, where I typically kicked off my shoes. The subtle smell the house inhabited was like a warm hug telling me I was home and the party had come to an end.

Tanner walked out from the hallway, his eyes grew large, and his brows peeked. "Bec!" He held his arms out wide, and I bounded into his embrace.

"Tanner! Oh my god! Let me look at you!" I pulled away. My eyes traveling the length of his body. His golden sandy hair and dark chocolate eyes. His sun-kissed skin led me to assume he'd spent his days outside soaking up the rays, and I was jealous. "Man! You look great! I can't believe how tall you've gotten!" A broad smile crossed his face, flashing with pride.

Easton appeared, and though it had been over a year and two lives of being with him, my stomach still fluttered.

"Hey! Wow! You're sunburnt!" He scanned my face and shoulders. "I mean, how was it?" Easton asked, grabbing me around the waist and planting a kiss on my cheek. I winced when his chin scrapped over my sensitive skin.

"It was so much fun. All of my friends came early so they could surprise me," I said, turning to Brooklyn. She stood in the doorway, hugging my pillow. "Oh, I'm sorry. Tanner, this is my friend Brooklyn," I said, motioning in her direction.

She smiled with a coyness that I'd never seen before, and my brows pinched in confusion. She slowly placed the pillow on top of my bag and took a step forward to meet Tanner. "Hello," Tanner said, shaking her hand. Her face flushed as she slid both hands into her back pockets. I turned to Easton, but he hadn't seen what I did. "God, Bec, I swear, if someone told me when I was eight years old that my brother would marry the girl next door, I sure as hell wouldn't have believed it!" Tanner chuckled. A smile appeared on Easton's face as he drew me in for another kiss. This time on the lips.

"You and me both, Tanner!" I said.

"Well, I should go. I know you have a lot to do." Brooklyn's voice was soft, and even though she was a sweet soul, her tone usually came off more confident.

"OK. I had a great time. Thank you!" I hugged her tight. She lingered for a moment before disappearing into the bright daylight in the front yard.

"So, how was the stripper?" Tanner asked., causing Easton to roll his eyes. "What?" he shrugged.

"He didn't hold a candle to you two handsome men . . . even in his thong," I said as the warmth spread across my cheeks.

"Ewww!" Tanner laughed, batting a hand in my direction.

Several wasted hours and one nap later, I made spaghetti for dinner. It was nice having Tanner around, as it reminded me of the old days. The days where all I cared about was how high I could jump on the trampoline. How famished I had become from running all day under the sweltering sun. And when I could see Easton next. The days where my biggest fear was what lay beneath my bed when the lights went out and the depth of the pool in the backyard. I longed for the time of my youth when I had not known of my cancer or the wreckage that stole my life. I wondered what would have happened if I never died and my cancer was cured. If Easton and I lived a long and happy life the first time around. I didn't know for sure, but I assumed I wouldn't have had the second chance at love that I was living now.

I watched Easton laughing with his brother over our small dining table for four, and I had never felt more at home. For all the things that had happened in my life, all the uncertainty and pain . . . it just made sense when I was with Easton. And seeing him with his brother made my heart feel whole again.

The boys looked at me expectantly, and the room grew quiet. My eyes pinged back and forth between them. ". . . I'm sorry, what?"

"The bachelorette party. How was it?" Tanner asked.

"Oh! Yeah." I nodded. "Well, I had thought that it was just going to be Brooklyn and me at the villa getting massages, but when we came back from the pool–"

"Now, is that where you got your third-degree burn? Or was that later on?" Tanner asked.

I said nothing but shot him a snarky look. He laughed like I imagined my brother would when he poked and prodded at me for the same reaction. Is this what it was going to be like? Was Tanner going to be like a brother to me? I guessed it made sense, after all, seeing as he was going to be my brother-in-law. "Like I was saying when we came back from the pool–"

"There was a naked guy in your room?" Tanner popped off again.

"Damn it, Tanner!" I snapped.

Easton and Tanner laughed, and I could tell that I had been outnumbered. I sighed before stabbing a meatball on my plate.

"OK. OK. I'm sorry. Continue, please," Tanner said.

"No."

"No. Come on. Come on. I'll be quiet."

"When we came back from the pool. . ." I said slowly, anticipating his next remark. When it didn't come, I continued, "Audrey, Grace, Kennedy, and Terra had driven down early to surprise me. And um, Payton was there too," I said. Easton was quiet, listening, waiting. Tanner bit his cheek. I continued cautiously, "We got massages, went wine tasting, had dinner . . . and then the stripper came–" I shook my head.

"Ahhh!" Tanner belted and laughed out loud. I shook my head, trying to dismiss it, but it lingered until the next topic was well under way.

"So, what are you doing these days, Tanner?" I desperately tried to maneuver away from the oil slick set of abs that had rolled mere inches away from my face. I knew we were all still thinking about it. But I prayed I was the only one envisioning it.

"Well, I'm an Interpretation Analyst. I do a lot of interpreting and a lot of analyzing, and–"

"You mean you sit on the couch all day playing video games?" It was my turn to fire off, and I intended to do so relentlessly.

Tanner's jaw dropped open, half insulted, half impressed at my quickness. "Uh, yeah. That's exactly what I meant when I said I was analyzing. . ."

"Oh my god!" I laughed. The banter extended well after dinner and flowed into the night. Tanner's affection for Easton was apparent, and if I hadn't of known any better, I'd have said that Easton was warming up to the idea of having him around for the week. It wasn't like Easton to get close to people, but he'd expressed to me that he wanted to change and that he was ready to open his heart, even if it meant hurting more in the end. He started taking Tanner's calls shortly after we got engaged. The boys talked on the phone about once a week until it had become second nature for Easton. I knew having Tanner stay with us was a big step for Easton, and I enjoyed watching him come around to the idea of family. I couldn't be more grateful that I was the girl who got to share her life with these two special guys. And I could feel that I was growing a chosen family around me. I knew Tanner was thankful for the opportunity to have his brother back in his life, too.

* * *

The seamstress pulled at the loose material around Grace's waist. Grace and Payton wore terracotta rust, Audrey and Brooklyn were in the cinnamon rose dresses, and Terra and Kennedy in the desert rose ones. All would hold mauve, cream, and mustard flowers, complementing the warm sultry tones in their dresses. They were stunning, each and every one of them.

Terra sat down on the sofa next to me in the fitting room. She handed me a mimosa, and we cheered our flutes together, causing a high pitch chime to echo in the air. "I know I give you a hard time about getting married at twenty-two, but I just want to say that I'm so happy for you. And I don't doubt your instincts for a second." Terra smiled at me, a tear forming in the corner of her eye.

"Aww, Terra. I know. Thank you," I said, squeezing her tightly.

Terra sniffed. "I can't wait to meet this mystery man. I mean, I know I'll love him, but still. I'm really looking forward to it."

"I can't wait!" I said, my jaw clenched tight with nervous energy. I'd been planning the wedding for a full year now. I knew it wouldn't be perfect—was such a thing even possible?—but I had been working tirelessly so that it would have the best chance possible. I loved Easton beyond this life, and I knew I wanted to marry him without a shadow of doubt. But would Grace's dress still pucker at the waist? Would my vintage bouquet appear dull and lack luster instead of muted? Because I specifically wanted it to look muted. And I knew it was going to be weird that Easton only had three people coming compared to my thirty-five . . . But *how* weird? Weird enough to ruin the ceremony?

"Becca?"

My eyes snapped to Maripat, the seamstress. I released my fingernails from the meat of my palms and stood to follow her into the dressing room for one last try on. The dress was stunning. It hugged my figure, showing off my curves. The back cut into a low v and flowed into a long lace train. I had Maripat add spaghetti straps to the mermaid fitted dress so I wouldn't have to worry about it slipping. The dress fit a little snugger than last time. Having fit like a second skin, I worried what would happen when we couldn't button it before the wedding.

"And you're still set on no veil? Correct?" Maripat asked. I nodded with a nervous smile. What if that was the wrong decision? "It looks beautiful," she said.

"Thank you. I love the straps. I would never have known the dress came without them." I traced the stitching with my fingertips.

"Thank you, dear. Now let's get you out of this dress, and you can join your friends."

The afternoon unfolded with paninis and tea at a favorite local eatery. The girls filled me in on the funny stories that had continued after the bachelorette party, spilling over to their stay at the nearest hotel. I struggled to stay engaged as the wedding was closing in. My mind raced, double-checking and triple-checking lists in my head. And when I had finally gone over every single worry in my head, I'd create new ones.

It wasn't me. I wasn't the type to turn into a monster as the wedding neared. But there was an undeniable shift that happened deep inside my mind as the prior forty-eight hours began counting down. My brain was dripping with worry, shorting out my circuits. Steam made of stress and anxiety expelled from my ears. I found it challenging to form complete thoughts as there was always a part of me stuck on the wedding. It wasn't until later that night that Easton called attention to it. Further expressing his perfect match for me, he helped ground me and wash away the worry. It was the stories of our past life that I loved hearing the most. I had some of my memory back, but I had never gained full clarity. The pieces I uncovered were still fuzzy and somewhat questionable.

"We married overlooking the Truly River. Well, we called it that, but there wasn't an officiant," Easton said. The fire casting a light show of shadow and highlight on the side of his face as we sat on the sofa.

"We didn't need anybody else," I said, recalling the need to marry before I was too sick.

"It wasn't for anybody else. It was just for us. And this wedding is no different," Easton said.

My gaze dropped to my fingers, entwined in the crocheted lap blanket. "I know."

"We're doing this for us, and as long as we're married at the end of the day, we will have succeeded," Easton said.

My brows lifted. He was right. He always was.

"Seriously! The building could burn down, the band could not show, and the cake could have a hair in it. Literally, everyone could get salmonella!" Easton's voice raised, "But if we walk out of there married. . .we've done it! Game over." Easton held his arms in the air, and I giggled. Letting a little stress roll off my back. "Right?" he asked.

"Yeah, no, you're right. But salmonella would be pretty bad—" I nodded.

"I know you, Beck. Don't you go adding food poisoning to your list of things to worry about. That's not what this conversation is about!" Easton warned.

He knew me so well. I mentally crossed it off the list. "I remember I ruined my dress. It was a white sundress. And by the time we left, it was trashed. I didn't care then. I don't know why I care now," I said, remembering the grass stains and rain-soaked sundress. It was one of the few memories I uncovered, and I held onto dearly.

"You had greater things to worry about back then. Hopefully, you can use that to put this wedding into perspective. We're getting married; that's all that matters. The rest is just a party. And you know what makes an epic party?" Easton asked.

"What?"

"Party fails," Easton shrugged.

I smiled. Eventually, it grew to show my teeth and beyond

into rolling laughter. "What's a party without party fails?" I shook my head in disbelief. It was a point of view I'd never considered and was glad to have looked upon now. We finished the night with ice cream and an hour of streaming party fails on TV. By the time I went to bed, I almost wanted to trip over my wedding dress and fall flat on my face. Almost.

CHAPTER 5

The wedding dress hung by the window sill and draped down to the floor. The warm glow of the sunrise behind it. Somehow, the lacy number represented the beginning of something new and yet, the continuation of something old all at the same time. I stood in front of it, the steam from my coffee warming my chin as I marveled over every ornate detail. The stitching was seamless, and the eyelet lace, intricate and mesmerizing. A rooster crowed in the far distance, bringing my focus back to me.

"I'm here! I'm here! Sorry, I'm late!" Brooklyn whirled into the room like a storm. Her dress draped over her arm as she balanced two coffees, her purse and a gift bag.

"No, you're right on time. I'm just early. I couldn't sleep."

"That's understandable," Brooklyn said as she unloaded her things. "Wow, it's really beautiful, isn't it?" she said, looking at the gown.

I smiled. Somehow calm after the last two days of

tension. I suppose it had finally run its course. Either that, or Easton's party fail pep talk did me right. "I want to remember this moment forever," I said as Brooklyn came to my side and locked her arm in mine.

"And you will," she said.

I shot her a sideways glance, and we both laughed. The thought of living forever was both exciting and daunting. I hadn't fully settled on which side of the fence I fell. Easton thought it was a curse, but my best friend found it to be a blessing. I wanted to be like her. I did. But every time I felt lucky to have a second chance, my stomach dipped with trepidation. Leaving me more confused than anything else. Sometimes I wondered if there was something that I failed to see or understand, and I feared it would swallow me whole when I realized it. When I finally saw the prison Easton had spoken of.

"It's your big day, Becca. You deserve this. Are you ready?" Brooklyn asked.

"Let's do it!" I said, beaming from head to pedicured toe. Whatever prison awaited me was neither now nor in my immediate future, so I pushed the worry down deep where it belonged. Because I had a wedding to celebrate.

A knock on the door startled me. Brooklyn checked her watch. "That's your beautician. Right on time. I already like her." Brooklyn crossed the room and opened the door. A man waltzed inside, carrying what I could only describe as a black toolbox. His black hair gelled like a hard helmet against his head.

"Oh my god! This ranch is stunning!" he said, his

cheekbones high and mighty, carved out with contour and highlight.

"Hi! Um, I thought Remy was coming?" Brooklyn said while glancing into the hallway.

"Honey, I am Remy!"

"Of course, I'm sorry. . ."

"Happens all the time," Remy waved dismissively. "Is this the bride? Oh, she is so burnt!" he exclaimed, setting down his things.

"Hi, I'm Becca Reed." I reached out to shake his hand, a little embarrassed.

"Soon to be Mrs. Green," Brooklyn added with a wink.

I settled in for what was scheduled to take one hour. I wanted all the glamour, but I still wanted to look like myself. But Remy had a plan, and I trusted him and his cheekbones to get the job done. He had a way about him that made me want to gush about everything. Easton, the wedding, girlfriend gossip. And I did. I don't think I stopped until he spun the chair around, and I came face to face with my reflection.

My heart skipped a beat. I couldn't believe that I was the very creature that looked back from my reflection. She was beautiful. And the best part was that I still recognized myself. Brows lifted, cheekbones more defined. The bow of my lip was exaggerated. And my eyes! My eyes were framed with just the right amount of shimmer and lash. Not overpowering my emerald eyes but enhancing their natural color.

"Remy! You're a genius! I love it!" I stammered as he pulled locks of my blond hair down to frame my face.

"Oh, honey! I'm so happy!" he placed both hands on top of his heart. A woman snapped candid pictures of the moment. I was so wrapped up in my ramblings to Remy that I hadn't noticed the photographer's arrival.

A sniff echoed behind me. "Mom! When did you get here?" I asked.

My mom stood in the door jamb, a tissue pressed under her nose. "Just now. Oh, baby, you look so beautiful!" she said. She came in for a hug, and I could sense Remy tense with worry that his masterpiece would smudge. Several snaps of the camera clicked like rapid fire. I wasn't used to being the center of attention, and it made me slightly uncomfortable. But if there were ever a time to receive so much attention, it was now, when my hair and makeup were crafted in to a masterpiece. I almost felt like a princess.

"I have something for you," Mom said, rummaging around in the depths of her purse.

"Oh yeah? You didn't have to get me anything, Mom."

"Well, technically, I didn't." Mom pulled out a small butterfly clip adorned with crystal chips. My heart swelled. "This was given to me when I was a little girl. Of course, I was never allowed to wear it. But I remember cherishing it from afar. I always imagined I would give it to my little girl one day." Her voice broke as she brought a tissue to her nose again.

Her eyes fluttered about, and only I knew she was reminiscing about how she never had that little girl, so she adopted me instead. I never talked to her about it after my first failed attempt. One moment slipped away, giving way to another chance that was also not perfect. By the time my

out when their hair was complete. The more of my bridesmaids that arrived, the more fun the pictures became.

"You still have time to run," Terra whispered in my ear. I whipped my head to face her right as the camera snapped. Was she still pressing this runaway bride thing? "*If* you wanted to," Terra shrugged.

"Thanks, but I'm good." It was the only thing I could think to say. My forehead creased, but the moment I remembered Easton's comments about party fails, I relaxed again and started counting. A rude comment from one of my closest friends was the first of many failures. I was sure of it.

Before I knew it, guests started to arrive. I parted ways with the bridesmaids, and the photographer and I walked back to the room across from the red barn where we would marry. I watched nervously out the window as the last guest trickled in as I waited for my dad. I hadn't seen him much since I moved to college, and it had been even less since he and my mom split. I knew it was going to be difficult for them to be together today.

The door creaked open, and my dad peered inside. "Dad!" I jumped up and wrapped my arms around his neck.

"Oh, Becca, you look beautiful in that dress!" His eyes scanned over me, and I blushed with pride.

"Thanks, Dad," I said.

"Are you ready to do this? You sure you want to marry the guy?" he asked sincerely.

"Dad! Why does everyone keep asking me that?"

"Well, dear, probably because you're twenty-two. You're just a baby!"

I tilted my head to the side, "I'm more grown-up than you realize, Dad," I said.

"Oh, I don't doubt that." Dad held his arm out, and I wrapped my hand around the crook of his elbow. We walked out to the side of the barn. The warm air soothed any residual nerves I had from before, and the smell of hay burned into my memory as a cherished moment. I'd probably think of my dad every time I smelled it from here on out.

I stepped on the front of my lace gown, propelling myself forward. My hand tightened around Dad's arm, and he was quick to grab ahold of me. I never hit the ground, but I did tear the front of my dress.

"Oh my god!"

"That was a close call!" Dad said.

"My dress is ripped!" I looked up with disappointment. My dress was not only ripped before I even managed to make it down the aisle, but the hem was dirty too.

"It's OK. Nobody will even notice." Dad's forehead creased, mimicking my worry. I nodded, looking back at the damage.

"Party fail number two," I said.

"What?"

"Oh! Did I say that aloud?" I took a deep breath. The music started, queuing me to walk down the aisle. "It's nothing," I said, smiling. I meant it. A ripped wedding gown was nothing if I walked off this ranch married to Easton.

My eyes lingered on my dad's warm brown eyes. They were not of my blood, but they were family. He loved me all the same, and I felt every morsel of it. I wrapped my arms around his neck and squeezed him tight as the music continued. "Thank you for being my father. Every day. Even when you didn't have to. Even on the days when I was difficult. And even now, after you and Mom split. I know I haven't always been easy to love, but you always made it effortless for me to love you back," I said, tears dampening my eyes.

Dad hugged me tightly. And I could tell by the second wave of emotion that poured out of him that he was beginning to wonder if I knew of the adoption. He pulled away, his body shaking, and smiled warmly. "I won't let you fall, dear. Ever . . ." For a moment, I thought he was about to say my actual name, Everly. I wondered what it would feel like if he had. Dad cleared his throat and straightened his back. He faced forward like a soldier ready for battle, and I joined him as we began the walk down the aisle together. Kicking my dress before planting each step, I knew even if I stumbled that my father would catch me.

CHAPTER 6

We rounded the corner of the barn, and I was met with a sea of hungry, attentive eyes. Each set was straining to get a glimpse of me as I walked down the aisle. It was more attention than I thought I could withstand, and I felt somewhat faint until my dad squeezed my arm, reminding me he was there to catch me should I fall. I scanned the crowd, recognizing faces I hadn't seen in some time but still meant the world to me. Friends from back home, aunts and uncles. Their warm smiles made my cheeks flush and my back heat. I looked back to the rip in the hem of my dress and took a deep quivering breath. Dad squeezed my arm. "You're missing the best part," he said, nodding to the alter.

I followed his gaze, almost afraid of the emotion that would pour out of me. I was barely holding on by a thread as it was, and I had only seen my distant friends and family. I knew that standing on that alter were my best friends. My closest companions. My soon-to-be brother-in-law. And the very love of my lives. My soulmate. And on a day like today, when my emotions were high, I had to take it all in, but in small segments. Pieces at a time, so that my heart wouldn't explode.

Muted mauve and cream flowers lined the alter. A beautiful halo of color around the man in black. My soon-to-be husband. He stood tall and confident. His typical dark, unruly hair had been tamed. I lowered my gaze from his hair to his eyes, where our gazes locked. I sucked in a quick and deep breath as if seeing him standing there was like fresh oxygen to my hungry lungs. As if he were the reason I could breathe again, and in a way, he was. His face, as he stood at the altar, was something I'll never forget. Awe-stricken. His mouth partly open. Eyebrows lifted, and eyes glassy. I could practically see his heart fluttering, and I knew mine had synced with his the moment our eyes met.

My life was just better with Easton. I didn't expect my friends to understand the depths of our relationship. How could they? And the feelings I had were not ones I could put into words. But if I had to choose a word to sum it all up, *lucky* is the only one close enough. I don't know how I ended up finding Easton on the side of the New River Bridge that stormy night, and I don't know how my soul survived my death, but I knew I was one lucky girl to have captured the heart of Easton Green.

My dad kissed my cheek and whispered, "I love you," in my ear. I smiled at him with a full heart before I took my place by Easton. His eyes fixed on mine as I took the steps alone.

"Dearly beloved, we are gathered here today to unite Easton Green and Becca Reed . . ." The words faded into the background as I stared into Easton's glacier blue eyes. My entire world right before me. The love I had for him created meaning beyond my wildest dreams. It was my second chance at my first love. And I was fortunate enough to see how it would have rightfully played out had I not been previously robbed of life. Robbed of my happily ever after.

Though standing in front of Easton, in my white gown, and in my second life; it truly was my second chance, and I owed it all to him. Without him, I doubt I would have been tethered at all. I would have had to live with some regrets. Some unlearned lessons. And essentially, a heart that never knew just how much it could love. Easton sucked in a deep breath and I caught myself doing the same. Mirroring his every move.

My eyes never left his as Brooklyn took my bouquet and Easton took my hands. "Becca. Beck. I'd like to say that I've waited a long time for my heart to find yours. But the truth is, I never knew love like this could exist. You've breathed new life into me, Beck, and I promise you today, and every day thereafter, that I will do my best to do the same for you." Easton lowered his gaze, clearing his throat. My stomach swam with anticipation and admiration. I squeezed his hands, not once, but twice. "In a world where love is the greatest power, and time is the most valuable currency, I vow to give you a very rich life. And I can't wait to spend my forever, with you by my side," Easton said, his tone soft like we were the only two people in the barn.

Awe-stricken, I choked back my tears. My chest tight as

my heart expanded. I took out the vows I'd written on a piece of paper. Hands trembling, I tried to steady the page. The words were a blur as tears filled my eyes. The only sound was that of the pounding of my heartbeat between my ears. I looked up from the fuzzy words into Easton's eyes and smiled. Tiny sparkles floated around him. Without looking, I knew it was his love bursting into the air like tiny fireworks.

I crumpled my vows into a ball and threw it over my shoulder, unable to speak. Leaping forward, I wrapped my arms around the nape of his neck and kissed him deeply. Easton grabbed me tight. My feet lifted off the ground as I deepened my kiss. I placed my hands on both sides of his cheeks as the distant sound of cheering erupted into my consciousness. I pulled back, laughing with embarrassment. A single tear rolled down Easton's cheek, and I swiped it away with my thumb. He lowered me onto the ground. And the officiant threw his notes behind his shoulder and tossed his arms up in the air. "I guess I pronounce you, husband and wife! And I'm sure you'll kiss the bride again," he said. And we did.

I turned to the crowd I'd forgotten were present, and Easton held up our intertwined hands. We laughed as they cheered, and Brooklyn gave me back my bouquet.

It was when we were taking photos that Easton caught my hand and slipped on the wedding band. Diamonds sparkled the full length of the band, making for quite the beautiful light show. "It's beautiful!"

"It's called an eternity band. I thought it was only fitting," Easton said.

"I love it!" I spun around, turning my back on Easton as I tried to fish his band out from my bust, but the slippery little thing kept slipping lower into my dress. "I can't . . . get it!" I spun back to face Easton. "I can't get it!" I laughed, rubbing the ring that was now pressed against my ribs. Thank God the dress was tight enough to hold it there. It shouldn't travel any lower.

Easton's eyes dropped to my neck line and then lower. His fingers traced mine over the ring. "I can't wait to get that ring tonight," he said in a hungry voice. My stomach dipped, and then even lower yet.

"OK, let's get another one by the tractor!" The photographer called out. Where did all these people keep coming from? My cheeks burned with embarrassment. I buried my face in Easton's chest, hoping to hide from the surrounding eyes. But when I heard the camera snap repetitively, I knew I was no longer safe. Easton's brother slapped his back, urging him toward the tracker.

"Come on, you two! You will have all week for that. I promise!" Tanner said.

"Can we leave now?" Easton asked.

"What! No! You guys can't leave now! The party hasn't even started!" Brooklyn said on my flank.

"Yeah!" Terra echoed.

I leaned into Easton and whispered quiet enough for only him to hear, "It will be worth the wait . . ." I said seductively.

"We heard that," Tanner said. I moaned, throwing my head back as the boys laughed. Easton squeezed my hand and winked. I knew I would be painted red in every single shot. Thankfully, I knew the photographer could fix that.

The pictures would have been awkward if they were with anyone else, but with this bunch, it was painless. Hysterical even. It was apparent that Tanner had been spending time with the bridesmaids because they all passed around a flask and shared an inside joke I was not privy to. I enjoyed seeing them together. I couldn't help but think Easton and I were making our own little family of tightly woven friends.

The MC introduced us as Mr. and Mrs. Green when we entered the larger barn set for dining and dancing. The sound of my new name sent a shiver of excitement down my spine. After being Everly Beck and Becca Reed, I'd held the name of Mrs. Green, and I loved it. It had been the easiest one to identify with that I could remember.

The wedding party took their seats. Easton and I in the middle, and some bridesmaids next to Tanner for balance. He didn't seem to mind, and neither did Grace and Kennedy by his side. However, I had to wonder about Brooklyn, who kept looking in his direction.

Even though I had been famished, I found it difficult to get down a quarter of my meal. A mixture of guests coming to our table to talk, the tightness of my dress, and nerves kept me from getting my fill. And when Brooklyn told me it was time to make my rounds, I abandoned my dinner altogether, for I knew it would grow cold.

I spoke to every table, and though I loved every moment, I couldn't help but be reminded of the wedding reception I never had in my past life. The one I somehow knew had happened and somehow saw my mom collapse under the news the cops had brought to my doorstep. Was this what it was supposed to be like? Would it have been this way, only with different faces? Or would they all have been too sad that I was terminal to be truly happy for me?

As I fought my past that never came to be, I was called to the dance floor for the father-daughter dance. A bolus formed in my throat, unable to swallow it down. And though I didn't cry, I knew my eyes were red from the burn. I almost scratched the father-daughter dance altogether. I knew it would hurt. I knew I'd have to be strong to get through it. But ultimately, I decided it was all a part of the healing process. Well, that and I couldn't take it away from my dad. He didn't deserve to be stripped from the father-daughter dance just because I missed my pop. I knew too that if I didn't do mine, then Easton wouldn't do his with his mother, and it would snowball into this thing that I was tired of overthinking. So, I told myself to suck it up. Be brave and fearless.

However, what I hadn't expected was the entire event had left me with very raw emotions. Memories that I hadn't even remembered until this night. And worse yet were the dreams. The ones that never came to be but haunted me in the mirrored moments of my parallel life. Riding side by side by a life that ended, I watched what could have happened unfold before my very eyes. And it was beautiful . . . But what I couldn't realize until this very moment was that the beauty hurt just the same as the sorrow.

"Just one step at a time, honey. Follow my lead," Dad said, taking me in his arms.

"Thank you, Dad," I said, forcing a smile.

He made small calculated steps, and I followed him, careful not to step on my dress again. I breathed in his cherry cigar smell that leached into his coat and was swept away in memories of him teaching me how to ride a bike. How to build a campfire. How to barbecue.

I was aware of all the eyes watching us but thankful for the dim lighting as my emotions were exposed for all to see. Front and center. I swallowed hard, actively pushing memories of my late pop out of my head. And then feeling guilty when I had succeeded. Feeling guilty when the happiness crept in. And when I felt the father's love of the man who danced in my pop's place.

I had kept it together. Locked it up tight. Buried it down deep . . . I had worked tirelessly to be strong, but when a song came on that my pop had sung to me as a kid—the only song he knew the lyrics to—I lost it. Completely and utterly lost it. Dad pulled me into his embrace as I wept. Wept for the dad who wasn't here to give me away. And then wept harder when I knew that, actually . . . he'd been here all along.

I opened my blurry eyes, lifting my head from my dad's shoulder, and looked around the room, expecting to see his face and those kind eyes that I'd missed so much. But when I couldn't see him, I closed my eyes once more, swaying back and forth to the slow song, basking in the feel of his presence, both far and near. His pride for me on this special day. And his deep unconditional, and undying love for me.

I basked in the glow of knowing the song Pop played was his gift to me. A present for me to know he's OK. And it was OK for me to be happy. Because this slow, steady song that played not only in my heart but for everyone to hear tonight. . . was *not* on my wedding play list.

CHAPTER 7

I wiped the wet tears off my cheeks as Easton and his mother stepped onto the dance floor. He looked at me with concern, but I forced a smile to let him know I was OK. I was *OK* . . . I *would be OK.*

The moment I stepped out of the limelight, Brooklyn took my arm and ushered me to the restroom. Grace had been waiting in the ladies' room for us and held the door open as we approached. "Are you OK?" Brooklyn asked. My eyes shot to Grace, and judging from her expression, perhaps my breakdown was worse than I even knew. I sniffed, my nose still running as I approached the sink. Startling myself as I looked into the mirror. *Three.*

This fail was epic: It could have counted as three *and* four. I looked like a raccoon from the smudged eye liner. My cheeks were not only missing make-up where I had wiped away my tears, but they were also exposing my residual sunburn and flaking skin. The only way to remedy this situation was to finish the rest of the wedding in the dark.

"Shit, you guys! What am I going to do?" I stared back at the girl in the mirror, and I was shocked to see that she looked nothing like the last reflection I'd seen before walking down the aisle. "Is Remy still here?" I asked.

The girls' eyes filled with worry, and I knew his shift was over long ago. The three of us sat in a moment of silence. Black mascara crumbled in bits that littered my under eyes. And though it had been waterproof, I had rubbed nearly all of it off my lashes. Brooklyn wet a paper towel and began to blot at my face. I let her take care of me as my eyes fell unfocused on the sink faucet. "What happened, Becca?" Grace asked.

My eyes flickered to Brooklyn, who most likely understood why I had broken down. "Oh, she . . ." She began a cover-up story like any true friend would.

"I recently found out I was adopted," I blurted out.

"Ohh!" Grace's eyes grew wide. She was not expecting that.

"And . . . that my biological father had just passed," I added. It felt good to get the truth off my chest. Even if there were parts that I still hid deep inside.

Grace threw a hand over her mouth. "I'm so sorry, Becca!"

"It's OK," I said. Though clearly it wasn't. I didn't know why it came out so dismissive as the proof was written all over my face that I was anything but OK. "The father-daughter dance was just . . . hard. That's all." I shrugged.

"Yeah, I can only imagine!" Grace said.

"But, I mean, nobody really noticed, right?" I asked, looking between Brooklyn and Grace. Their eyes met for a second before they agreed in unison.

"Yeah!"

"Right! Yeah."

I sighed. Grace couldn't lie to save her life, and I knew Brooklyn too well to know she was only trying to make me feel better. Brooklyn opened a small cosmetics bag and worked her magic. When I looked back in the mirror, I looked nothing like the girl I had when Remy made me up. But at least, I was presentable. Sort of. "Thank you," I said, hugging them both.

"You know you can talk to us, anytime," Grace said. I smiled at her. Wishing that I could. That my secrets weren't so out of this world that I had to keep them locked inside. Maybe then I wouldn't have melted down in front of all my wedding guests.

"I will. Thank you," I said with no intention of ever telling her I was on my second life, and of all the pressures I carried on my shoulders to make it better than my first one.

By the time we had re-entered the barn, the party had kicked up a notch. I was glad to see that my breakdown was all but forgotten, and everyone was enjoying themselves. I found Easton standing awkwardly with both of our parents near the back wall. I straightened my back, sucked in a breath of confidence, and strode over to them. Easton reached out far before I was in arm's length, willing me to hurry by his side.

"There she is!" Easton's dad reached out to hug me. Followed by a warm embrace from his mother. I knew they saw my episode on the dance floor, but I was more than OK pretending nothing happened.

"Hi, thank you for coming," I said.

"Oh! We wouldn't have missed this for the world!" Easton's mother said.

"I see you've met my parents." I smiled.

"Yes! We just met, Mr. and Mrs. Reed."

My mom looked down at the ground, rubbing the back of her neck. My dad flinched, opening his mouth but ultimately closing it without correction. They were newly split after a long stint of trying to make their marriage work. In the end, my dad felt he could no longer trust my mom for cheating on him. And as I would internalize it, I seemed to think it was my fault for walking in on her. Though I knew it wasn't. It had nothing to do with me at all. Except, perhaps, that the only reason my mom confessed to sleeping with her art instructor was because I had found out. Either way, it was a big step for them to be here tonight, standing next to each other. Cordially. And I had faith that if I could survive the father-daughter dance, they could survive this awkward night together. If not for themselves, then for me.

"Hey, you doing OK? You seemed . . . It seemed rough out there?" Mom asked.

My eyes flickered to both sets of parents before landing on Easton's calming gaze. "Yeah. I'm going to be OK," I said before returning my gaze to her. "Just a moment of reflection, I guess," I said. The parents nodded understandingly. Or so they thought. I caught my dad's eyes as he was trying to evaluate my mother's expression, and I assumed he was wondering if she knew that I had knowledge of the adoption. Her face showed no telltales.

The MC came on to the speaker, announcing that a few guests had requested to make speeches and asked everyone to take their seats once again. My stomach churned as I said goodbye to both sets of parents and headed for my seat. Once there, Easton held my hand on his lap. "Are you OK?" he whispered, leaning in.

"Yeah, I'm OK." I nodded. But when the concern didn't leave his face, I followed up with, "Seriously, I'm OK."

Tanner took the stage, looking incredibly nervous. The microphone shrieked, and the audience recoiled, causing me to giggle into the back of my hand. He wiped his palms on his slacks. "I feel like you all have been hearing a lot of positive, loving things about Easton and Becca over the last couple of nights. So . . . buckle up," Tanner flipped his note card, and my face grew warm. The crowd laughed, eager to hear the roasting. My nerves flared.

"Oh, shit. . ." Easton muttered, amused.

"I just want to start by saying how beautiful Becca looks tonight. Doesn't she look beautiful?" The crowd clapped, looking back at me, and my stomach dropped. A smile spread across my face. I was going to kill him when I had the chance. "And so do all of Becca's friends and bridesmaids. They all look really, really beautiful! Really, stunning—did I say that I was single?" The crowd laughed, and Brooklyn reached over and grabbed my leg, squeezing it with a firm grip. Excitement passed through her eyes.

Did she really like him? Brooklyn was never phased by guys.

"It may come as a surprise to you all that Easton and I are adopted." Easton went rigid by my side, but my eyes immediately flicked to my mother, who at that moment looked to me as well. My stomach somersaulted. Even from across the room, I could see in her face that she was calculating the reason I looked to her during that very statement. I would have to talk to her soon but now was not the time.

"That's the reason why I got the looks, and he . . . well, he looks like that." The crowd laughed, and even Easton broke. He leaned forward, placing his elbows on the table as he engaged in his brother's speech. "After bringing Easton home, my parents said, 'He's so wonderful. We want another,' which is how I came to be in the Randolf family. Randolf, you ask? Yes, Easton changed his name when he legally could at eighteen so that it would match his birth certificate."

Worried eyes began to look back at our table, and I slowly leaned into Easton and muttered, "Four . . ."

"Four what?" he asked, never taking his eyes off Tanner.

"Four wedding fails."

"Has there been four already?" Easton asked, raising his eyebrows.

"Yes, but this has potential to turn into multiples," I said, smiling back at everyone. Easton laughed and leaned over to kiss my cheek.

"Three moments stick out in my memory I'd like to share with you about Easton tonight. The first is when he tried to drown me in ice cream when we were young," Tanner said, flipping his note cards.

"Good god, he's still going," Easton muttered, shaking his head.

"You see, I had become too much of a treat. With my dashing looks and all," Tanner said, causing the bridesmaids, in particular, to giggle. Tanner was quite a looker, and perhaps that was what made it so uncomfortable. "But Easton never had to worry about being second best, because he was the true shining star of the Randolf household. But even though he had the brains, Easton saw it fit to eliminate his competition. Thankfully for me, he didn't have the muscle for it, and I survived the first attack." Tanner took a moment to let everyone quiet down before he continued. I peeked over at Brooklyn, who practically had stars in her eyes. The way she looked at Tanner on stage nearly made me blush.

"The second memory I have is when he would teach me math until my brain would explode. Seriously, it exploded all the time. And at that point, Easton would just do the work for me so that we could go play. Sorry, Mom!" I laughed, and Easton nodded, confirming the story to be true.

"But the third memory that sticks out in my mind, even more than when he tried to kill me in my lactose rich dessert, and still, more than when he pushed me to be a better man . . . And ultimately giving up on me . . . was when a little girl moved in next door." Tanner said, and my heart warmed. My friends and family started to look back at me once more, as this was not a story many of them had heard.

"You see, this was no regular little girl. She was fun! Even when she wore too much pink. She and Easton became best friends, and I often stayed home while they played to finish my homework. Funny how Easton stopped doing my homework when he saw how that played out for him, huh?" The crowd laughed. I pinched my cheeks, which were on fire.

"Yup, you'd never believe that Easton found his wife at eight years old. But he did." Friends and family looked around, shocked. My parents and closest friends nodded, confirming it was, in fact, a true story. I smiled, thinking they didn't know the half of it.

"Easton told me so after the very first day he met her; he said that he would marry her. I thought he had finally gone crazy, but it actually happened. Just three short weeks later! Yup, I have the picture to prove it! Officiated by a rabbit, but nonetheless, they married in her backyard that summer. And when we moved away—and Easton did my homework again, no surprise there—Easton's heart broke a little. You see, he never gave up looking for his bride!"

The crowd awed, and I leaned over to kiss Easton on the cheek. He moved swiftly, and our lips met. "No girl was good enough for Easton in high school. Or so he said. He matured late, and I see his muscles have yet to come in. But hey, your voice finally dropped, am I right, buddy?" Tanner gave Easton a thumbs up, causing Easton to sink into the seat a little. I lost it, laughing so hard I was sure my cheeks would cramp. Easton chuckled, shaking his head at his brother, then slowly and reluctantly returned his thumbs up. Tanner continued.

"So, I'll wrap this story up for those of you who don't know it. Easton changed his name and moved out of the Randolf household as soon as he was legally allowed to do so. Soon after that, he stopped taking our calls and basically vanished. Until one day, some three years later, he called to tell me he found his bride." I placed my hand over my heart as it melted in my chest. I'd never heard this side of the story.

"And slowly, from that day on, Easton started answering his phone when I would call. He came back into my life, and I don't think that would have happened if it weren't for his lady here. So, let's raise our glasses," Everyone raised a glass of champagne. "And cheers to the fact that Easton was too wimpy as a kid to drown me in a bowl of ice cream!" I nearly spit out my champagne. "Oh, and cheers to Becca too, because I think she's pretty great!" I clapped ferociously, standing up. Easton rose to his feet too and started a slow clap. I loved every second.

I stood when Tanner approached our table and kissed him on the cheek. The smell of Tequila strong on his breath. I wondered how much he had to drink to deliver his speech and how far he veered from his original one. Easton slapped his back while he gave him a quick embrace. He said something in Tanner's ear as I placed my chilly hands on my warm cheeks, trying to massage out the tension from laughter. "Oh, I can't wait until he gets married," Easton muttered. And I laughed all over again. Only stopping when I noticed my mom had taken the stage.

"Hello, everyone. What a wonderful speech, thank you. Um, I'm Becca's mom. Um, wow, this barn must have a great antenna because this is a great reception!" A bark lodged in my throat, making a weird sound as I grabbed Easton's leg underneath the table. Few laughed, but mostly out of discomfort. I bit my lip, waiting for her attempt to recover.

"Um, well, I've been preparing this toast for a long time now, so I hope it's not burnt!" Mom said.

"Oh, no!" escaped me. Easton burst out in laughter as my mom looked frantically around the room. Second-hand embarrassment had never been so real.

"Becca is such a beautiful daughter. Loving and kind. She's the kind of girl you don't worry about introducing to your parents. That's why she didn't introduce us to Easton's parents until twenty minutes ago. . ."

I shot Easton a look, and we both said it. "Five!"

"Five, this is definitely number five!"

The speech went on in what was intended to be not only funny but loving. Very loving. It just never quite went anywhere at all. Not before my dad interrupted with a speech of his own. And he could only get a few words in before breaking down and crying into the microphone. And it didn't end there. No, speeches came from many of my bridesmaids, too. But the best one came from Brooklyn, which wasn't a speech at all, but a complete shutdown.

"Thank you for all the lovely speeches. Now, if I could get all the single ladies up here, Mrs. Green is going to throw the bouquet!" she took the microphone with her, which I could only secretly thank her for. I'd have to tell her how much I loved her for that when the time was right.

"Thank god that's over!" I laughed, shielding my face behind my hand. "My poor parents!" I said.

Easton laughed, "Please tell me someone got that on video!" Easton peered around the room, "Are we having this taped?" he asked.

"No, probably should have, though."

"Go throw your bouquet. Let's see if we can get number six," Easton said, nudging me out of my seat.

I chuckled, standing up. I grabbed my bouquet of muted mauves, off whites, and mustard yellow flowers. It was every bit the vintage look I was going for. I hated to throw such a beautiful bouquet, but I couldn't argue with tradition.

I stood with my back to the bridesmaids and a few other women, mostly young. I was happy to see my mom hadn't joined. "One, two, three!" I threw the flowers over head with as much might as I had. A loud thud sounded, followed by gasps from the crowd. I spun just in time to see flower petals floating down from the large industrial-sized fan. Mustard, mauve, and cream petals began to litter the dance floor. In the tragedy's wake, it was almost beautiful.

A moment of stillness passed before someone screamed, "It's mine!" and took off running to the back of the barn where the bulk of the bouquet had spat from the fan. My eyes met Easton's as a dozen single ladies ran to the back of the room. Two toppled over each other. Chairs were knocked over, and a table cloth pulled, sending several glass champagne flutes crashing to the ground. A few grunts ensued before Payton raised her arm high and mighty, thrusting the tattered bouquet into the air. About a third of the flowers were missing, leaving cut stems in their place, but surprisingly, the rest had held up pretty well. I clapped as Grace pulled Terra off the floor. I snickered and held six fingers up to Easton from across the room.

CHAPTER 8

Six wedding fails. That's how many it took to make the perfect wedding. By the time the sparklers were lit and our friends and family formed a tunnel for us to pass through, Easton and I were ready to take our love somewhere more private.

"Ready, Mrs. Green?" Easton asked, taking my hand.

"Ready!" I said, grabbing as much of my lace dress as possible and lifting it off the ground. We sprinted through the sparklers, a beautiful whirlwind of bouncing, flickering lights. And by the time we reached the end of the tunnel, Tanner and Brooklyn had shaken champagne bottles and popped them over head. Champaign rained down on us, taking me back to the clearing that overlooked the Truly River on the evening we first wed. I looked to Easton as we ran to the car, and I wondered if he had lived in the constant realm of déjà vu, in how I had today.

Easton opened my door, and I crawled into the back seat. Scooping my lace train off the ground before closing the door. Easton ran around the back of the car. With a slam of his door, we were one step closer to finally being alone. The driver pulled away, and I kissed Easton's champagne-soaked lips as the wedding cans clanked behind the car. We watched the glow of the sparklers disappear into the night as the wedding had finally come to an end. "Success!" I said.

"It really was," Easton said. "But the best is yet to come."

I raised my brows. "That's a big promise," I said.

"Well, as you may have heard . . . I eventually hit puberty so . . ." I giggled, causing Easton to wag his brows. We spent the rest of the ride to the airport caught between lusting over each other or laughing at something that had happened at the wedding. And in no time, we were waiting to board the plane.

Several people had come up to us saying "Congratulations," because I was the only one in the whole airport wearing a wedding gown as far as I could see. I itched to take it off, but I feared it might be cutting it too close. And missing our flight was one wedding fail that I didn't want to come to fruition.

"I don't know how we got here so late. I thought we were good on time," Easton said, checking his watch.

"I think our flight moved up to an earlier slot. We should have checked it this morning," I said, gripping my luggage handle and yanking it off the train of my gown.

"Should have. Guess I was too excited to see you in this dress to think about it," Easton said, his eyes trailing down my figure. I smiled.

"Congratulations! You look so pretty!" A woman said as she passed by.

"Thank you!" I said, blushing. "I need to get out of this dress," I hissed to Easton.

"Flight 3838, ready to board!"

Easton looked at me with large, round eyes. "Do you think you have time?"

I looked nervously to the passengers lining up for the flight and then back down the way we came in. Not only were the restrooms far away, but I doubted I could take the dress off by myself. "I don't think so! What am I going to do? I can't wear this thing for a nine-hour flight! I'm suffocating as it is!" I fanned my face, feeling the panic rise.

"It's OK. No worries. You can take it off on the plane." I shot him a look of doubt, causing him to follow up with, "I promise. I'll help you." I nodded. Unconvinced, but accepting that I had no other choice. We got in line, and it moved swiftly. My suitcase rolling over the lace train of my dress again. Easton bent over and picked it up, holding it while I walked. "See, I can help!" he said. I smiled, thankful for all he did.

We funneled onto the plane, taking our seats over the wing. Easton placed our luggage overhead, and I sat next to the window. "Do you want to take it off now?" he asked.

I looked around. People were still filing onto the plane. "I don't think we're supposed to use the bathroom until the plane gets in the air," I said. Easton took a seat next to me and patted my leg. "Thanks, but . . . I can't wait fifteen more minutes," I told him.

Ten minutes later, and I couldn't wait any longer. The

plane hadn't even begun to move, and I was on the verge of hyperventilating. "I've got to take it off!" I said, standing. Not a single thought could process through my head if it didn't involve ripping this corset off and freeing my lungs. I made it to the back of the plane before getting turned around by the flight attendant.

"I'm sorry, there's nothing I can do. You have to wait until the plane is in the air and the seatbelt lights have turned off," the flight attendant said. I nodded, taking quick, shallow breaths on my way back to my seat. Of course, being afraid of flying wasn't helping my situation. I would have been nervous normally, but it was the dress that made me feel claustrophobic. I placed my hand on my stomach and tried to slow my breathing.

"What's wrong?" Easton asked by the time I got back to my seat, still wearing the dress.

"They won't let me in the bathroom!" I crawled over him and plopped down in my seat. He gathered the train of my dress and pulled it out of the walkway, pooling it at my feet.

Easton took out the brown paper bag in the seat pocket before us. "Here, breath into this." I protested with my bulging eyes, not wanting to look more ridiculous than I already did. "Just do it!" he said. I followed his orders and began breathing in the bag.

The flight attendant came by and slipped me two bottles of vodka. "Don't tell anyone. I'm not supposed to hand these out. But it should take the edge off."

"Thank you," Easton said, taking the bottles. I continued breathing into my brown paper bag, and Easton handed me an uncapped bottle. My eyes scanned his in question. "She's right. It'll help," he said.

I lowered the bag and sucked down the bottle. Barely able to swallow it all, I coughed as a shiver split down my spine. Easton smiled. "Stop it!" I snapped. My eyes darted to the second bottle. "That one too!" I reached over him, taking the drink from his hand. The clear liquid was even worse the second time, and my reaction was no better. Aftershocks ripped through me like jolts of electricity. Easton smiled, trying hard not to laugh. "Stop that!" I said, picking up the brown bag again and placing it over my mouth.

Eventually, the plane lifted off the runway. The force pressed me back in my seat, adding even more pressure to my anxiety-ridden chest. My nails dug into Easton's forearm as he rattled off the most ridiculous statistics I'd ever heard. "Did you know that you are seven times more likely to die of a paper cut than to crash in a plane? And nearly thirty times more likely to witness a real-life mermaid?" He said in all seriousness.

"What?" I crumpled my paper bag, finally able to breathe. My thoughts were consumed with mermaids as the claustrophobia fell to the wayside. How much had I drunk again? Because one of us was crazy, and I didn't want it to be me. By the time the seatbelt lights turned off, I was in a different mindset altogether. The fear had become amusing, and the tightness of my dress only a game.

"Hey, Easton?" I asked. He leaned in, looking up at me from underneath his lashes. "I don't think I can get this dress off by myself. You're going to need to help me." The looped buttons were far too complicated for me to manage behind my back. And in a moving cabin, it would be impossible.

"Sure, anything I can do to help." Easton peeked at the back of the plane before turning back to me. "You go first, and then I'll slip in behind you when no one's looking," he said.

I nodded. Every single pair of eyes lifted to me as I passed through the aisle. It was like walking down the aisle in the barn, only this time I didn't have my father's strength beside me, and the eyes that stared back were neither proud nor loving. They were strangers, and I had no idea what they were thinking. All I knew was that I needed to get out of this wedding dress as soon as possible. I tightened my grip on the change of clothes in my hand.

I opened the cabin door and stepped inside. But before closing the door, I saw the lace of my dress's hem peeking out from under the door. I bent down to pick it up, but the other restroom across the aisle caught my eye. What if Easton had walked into the wrong stall? I smiled, almost wanting to see it happen. But then I left the lace closed the door. This way, there would be no mistaking. I turned to look at myself in the mirror. My hair had not budged one bit from the ceremony, but my makeup had done several things. My lips were bare and lashes naked. I suddenly became more self-conscious for all the thoughts that passed through the passengers' heads as I walked by.

A light tap rapped on the door before opening. Easton pushed his way in as quick as a storm. His chest pressed up against mine in the tiny stall, and I felt my heart quicken.

My eyes searched his, mere inches from his face. "Uh, it's a little tight in here," he said.

I tried to take a step back, but my heels hit the base of the toilet. The front of my dress yanked me forward. "You're standing on my dress," I said, trying to look down.

Easton picked up his foot but had nowhere to go. He grabbed handfuls of my gown and tried lifting it out from under his feet, nearly knocking me over in the process. I burst out into laughter, and Easton cupped his hand over my mouth. "Shhh. We have to be quiet," he whispered. His eyes locked on mine with conviction, but I was far more guilty than being too loud. A smile spread across my face that I could no longer hide.

"Hey, have you ever heard of the mile high club?" I asked in my most seductive tone. A tone that I was sure could only come out after taking shots on an empty stomach.

"No. Don't start that. We have to get you out of the dress and then get back to our seats. Can you turn around?" Easton asked.

"Would you like that?" I asked, dropping my shoulder.

"Beck . . ." Easton warned.

"Yes . . ." I bit my lower lip.

"Turn around!" Easton said, not having any of it.

"Ugh, fine!" I tried to spin, but Easton was still on my dress. I nearly toppled over. My hand slammed against the back wall and Easton's hands tightened around my waist, catching me. Bent over, I turned slowly, giving it one last try. I winked at him. As sexy as I could wink, I did. But when both my eyes closed, I had to try again . . . and again. Why couldn't I wink? I thought everybody could wink?

"Beck! Please!" Easton begged. I couldn't tell if he was annoyed or just taking pity on me, but maybe it was a bit of both.

"Jesus! Is there nothing I can do to turn you on?" I demanded.

"Beck, you don't have to try to turn me on. This just isn't the place or the time. Damn it, how do you take this thing off?" he hissed.

"But, mile high club . . ." I whined.

Easton stilled. The air shifted, growing thick with lust. I knew I had it in me to seduce him. When he couldn't hold himself back any longer, he slowly leaned forward, his breath hot against the nape of my neck. "Is that what you really want?" he whispered.

My breath quickened. I was in no position to make decisions. But something inside of me screamed for me to live my life, and I was pretty sure it was the alcohol. "Yes!" I gasped.

Easton planted a wet kiss on the back of my shoulder, sending shivers down my spine. I lifted my head, exposing my neck, and he trailed his mouth up to my ear. My hand tightened around the base of the sink, and my head began to swim.

"Take off the dress!" I said in a breathy, needy voice.

Easton undid the uppermost buttons from the corset, and I could expand my lungs for the first time since slipping on the dress. I sucked in a deep, much-needed breath of air. He lifted the gown from the floor, bumping into me. I laughed out loud as I nearly fell into the toilet. "Shhh," Easton said from behind as he stifled his own laughter. I gripped the top of my corset and yanked it down with as much force as I could, freeing myself from the tightness and suffocation.

A glisten of gold flickered from my bust, dropping into the toilet bowl below with a splash. I went rigid. "What was that?" Easton asked, bumping into my back and pushing me forward to get a look over my shoulder. His body pressed against mine, forcing me to take a step forward. Tripping, my hands hit the back wall once more. Only this time, one of my hands landed squarely on a button, pressing it until the toilet flushed fiercely. I watched Easton's wedding band vanish in a violent vortex below. My heart stopped.

"What? What was that?" Easton repeated, still arching over my shoulder. Turbulence struck, and the lights flickered on and off. I pushed my hands into either side of the cabin walls, trying to hold on. The lights went completely out, and my heart pounded in my chest. Then, in the blackness of the cabin, a knock rapped on the door.

"Ma'am, you're going to have to go back to your seat. The seatbelt light is back on. Ma'am?"

"Shit!" I said, tugging at my dress.

"Ma'am!"

CHAPTER 9

After a long sleepless night on the plane, we landed on the main island of Tallaway. The sun had recently risen, but already the air was warm and thick with humidity. We were ushered through security and placed in the back seat of a taxi, our belongings in the trunk. The island of Taiseen was a thirty-minute boat ride from the main island.

"Welcome to Tallaway!" Our driver said.

"Thank you, sir," Easton said before his eyes settled on me. "How are you holding up?" he asked.

A tired smile spread across my face. "I didn't sleep very well on the plane. But other than being sleepy and a little embarrassed, I'm good," I said, my wedding dress draped across my lap.

"You're still embarrassed? Why? Don't be . . . You're never going to see those people again," Easton promised.

"Yeah, you're right. I just wish I didn't have to walk

back to my seat with a half unbuttoned wedding dress!" I let out a huffing laugh. "You should have seen the stares they gave me!" My eyes lost focus in the memory.

"Oh, I know. I got them too," Easton said. I giggled because it took a lot to embarrass him. He was usually so set on not making a fool of himself and denying his desires in that miniature bathroom. I think that walk of shame did him in though, and it was almost worth it to see the flush in his cheeks.

Easton paid the driver, and he helped us load our bags onto the boat. My cheeks painted red when I realized the small boat was occupied with not only us but two other couples from the plane. My eyes dropped the second I remembered them, and I hoped they hadn't recognized me outside of my wedding gown. . . The wedding gown I carried before me.

Once Easton sat by my side, my eyes lifted ever so slightly to the couples. Both the men were playing with their new wedding bands. I lifted my head to Easton and leaned into his ear. "Never going to see them again, huh?" I whispered. His eyes left mine to look at the other passengers. I knew the moment he recognized them when his face flushed crimson. His eyes dropping to the bottom of the panga.

"Are you guys honeymooning on Taiseen, too?" One of the men asked.

"Yeah, man. Congratulations!"

Easton cleared his throat. "Yeah, we'll be there as well. All week. Congratulations to you guys as well," he said. I smiled at the other women.

between my toes. I closed my eyes and tilted my head up to the sun. The sun rays kissed my face, and I smiled with open arms.

"Mmm," I hummed.

"I know, right?" Easton said.

"I cannot believe this place," I said.

"You haven't even seen the best part!" He pulled on my arm. I reached down to grab my shoes.

"I don't know what could be better than this? Honestly, I could park it right here in the sand and be the happiest girl all week long."

"Wife," Easton corrected me with a smile. It still sounded weird, and I wondered how long it would take to get used to hearing it. We stepped onto the dock and strolled slowly to our overwater bungalow. I ran my hands down the wood railing as my eyes searched for movement in the water. "I think six is at the end," Easton said. The panga's engine started, and it idled away slowly. When we reached the end of the dock and stood at the doorway of the sixth bungalow, Easton turned to me with a wicked smile. He bent down and scooped me up in his arms. I wailed in laughter as we burst over the threshold.

I squealed, delirious from lack of sleep and the emotional last twenty-four hours. Easton kicked the door closed behind him and took me straight to the bed. He unloaded me, throwing me into the air. I landed on top of a white feather comforter as soft as a cloud. My eyes flickered around the room, taking in my surroundings, but Easton was quick to jump on top of me. I squealed once more before his kiss silenced me, and my focus zeroed in on him and him alone. No more wedding fails, no more plane passengers, no more missing ring; just me, my husband, and this bed.

I arched my hips into his. My hands grew greedy as I grasped and clawed at his back, pulling his shirt off. He planted a kiss from the neck down to my tattoo as I squirmed, kicking off my clothing. I don't know how long we spent showing each other our love, but when I saw it manifest before my very eyes in a warm glowing light between us, I knew that we were making the best of our time on the Taiseen island.

My heart still pounding, I smiled, and the warm tears of joy streamed down my cheeks. I brought my fingertips to the corner of my eyes and blotted my tears. "Are you OK?" Easton asked, his hand tangled in my hair.

I didn't know why I was crying, but the tears that sat on my fingers before my eyes couldn't be mistaken. "Yeah, I think I'm just . . . I don't know? I think I'm just . . . happy?" I said. What else could it have been? I had been so tightly wound with the wedding, and then the airplane incident. I guess being here with Easton was like shedding pounds of fear, worry, and anxiety. And better yet, it was all sinking in. He was my . . . *husband.* I had him for the rest of my life, for the rest of . . . *time?* "I'm sorry, that's really weird isn't it?" I asked.

Easton stroked my hair. "No, it's not weird," he said. I turned to him with loving eyes, and when a smirk escaped him, I grabbed the nearest pillow and thrashed it into his face. "What? What? It's a little weird, but I accept you for you!" Easton cried out through laughter.

I giggled, wiping away the rest of my overly emotional tears, and hopped to my feet. I pulled on my lounge clothes that had been tossed clear across the room and ventured out into the bungalow. The teak wood creaked as I walked to the middle of the living room and looked down through a window on the floor. The aqua blue water lay beneath. "Did you see this?" I looked back to Easton, who was still sprawled on the bed with his eyes closed.

"See what?" He pulled himself up and came to my side. Slowly, I placed one foot on top of the window. When it felt sturdy enough, I put my full weight on the glass. I smiled at Easton, and he grabbed my hand, pulling me to the slider door. "If you think that is cool, check out the deck." Easton slid the door open, and warm, briny air rushed inside the villa. A large deck opened up over the water. Our very own dock. Two lounge chairs and a ladder leading straight into the water.

"Stop it!" I said in amazed disbelief. "I don't know how I'm ever going to leave this place! You spoiled me!" I said, crawling into the lounge chair. "I'm so tired. I could fall asleep right here! But I don't want to miss a thing," I said before I closed my eyes, truly not wanting to miss a single second of this stunning island. When a splash sprayed me, my eyes flew open, and I nearly hopped out of the lounge chair.

"Wow, Beck! It's so warm! You have to come in!" Easton called out.

"I can't just jump in the ocean," I said, wanting nothing more than to be carefree like he was.

"Why not?"

"I don't know?" I looked around nervously. There wasn't a soul in sight. "What about sharks? And stuff?" I asked.

"Beck, if you don't get in this water, I'm coming up there. And you don't want to know what will happen if I do," Easton said before ducking under the water and disappearing from sight. I sighed, not knowing what was holding me back. Other than me, that was. I was always the one holding me back. But I didn't want that anymore. I pulled my shirt off and shimmied out of my joggers, exposing my white lace bra and matching panties. I took one more look around, and when the coast was clear, I ran and jumped off the dock, letting out a small scream before I hit the lukewarm water with a splash. My body submerged for only a few seconds, but it was long enough to bring back the fear of drowning in the river. As quick as I jumped in, I swam back to the ladder and climbed up the dock. Easton splashing me as I did.

"What? I did it!" I said.

"Yup, you sure did," Easton said before he swam to the steps after me. I couldn't tell if he was serious or if it was my own guilt for not being more of a free spirit that sat unsettled in my stomach, but I buried it, either way. This wasn't a place of worry, and I wouldn't let myself get me. I padded into the bungalow with wet feet and fetched us two towels. "Thanks," Easton said after I handed him one.

We dried off before curling up in the lounge chairs and staring out amongst the crystal clear water. Neither of us said much, and I imagined his eyes were closed before mine had finally lost their long battle. Lulled to sleep by the sounds of the lapping water, we slept until nearly noon. And even then, when we woke, I wasn't convinced I had ever stopped dreaming. Life was as beautiful as the island of Taiseen, and I had unlimited time to experience all of it. We did, together.

CHAPTER 10

Day two of our honeymoon and the slow hum of relaxation had fully sunk in. My breathing had deepened, my heartbeat grew to a steady rhythm, and my thoughts quieted. Island life was good for me, and I had already promised myself I would come back. Not just to this island, but all of them. Easton and I would explore every island on this green earth. I didn't care if it took hundreds of lives; it was my first Tethered Soul goal, and it made my heart sing with excitement.

"The sand is so white and fine here," I said, peering out behind my coffee mug to the white beach beyond.

Easton looked down to his bare feet and dug his toes under the sand. "It's beautiful," he said leisurely.

"Do you think they're all like this? All the islands?" I asked.

"No. Some will have brown sand. Some won't have any sand at all. Just shells or small pebbles. You've never been to an island before?" Easton asked.

"Not before this. . . I could live like this forever," a low hum sounded from my throat and my eyes closed for a brief moment, taking in the perfect day.

"It's about to get even better. Want to know what I have planned for today?" Easton asked.

My eyes fluttered with anticipation, and I set my coffee down in my lap. "What's that?" I asked. Easton's excitement brought a smile to my face. If he was this excited, I already knew it would be perfect.

"Skydiving!" he exclaimed.

Coffee spewed from my mouth and misted my legs. Fear froze my mind, and not a single thought had passed as my once calm heartbeat kicked into a gallop. "What?" I asked though I knew I had heard him correctly.

"Skydiving?" Easton replied. His tone, once excited, was now laced in trepidation. He paused, waiting for my reply. A sign of some sort that I was going to be alright. But when it didn't come, he continued. "You may not remember, but in your first life, we had an agreement of sorts. You didn't have long to live, and there were things you had wanted to do . . . to experience. We made a list, and we crossed items off the list as we went. There are still items we haven't crossed off," Easton said.

"I know that! But . . . I don't recall skydiving being one of them!" I said as I wiped the coffee droplets off my legs with a napkin. The truth was, I probably didn't remember half of the things we put on that list.

Easton quieted. "Well . . . technically. . . it wasn't. But it is really close to bungee jumping! And that one *was* on your list."

"Are we really bringing that back up?"

"Well, you didn't get a chance to experience it? So, it's back on the list," Easton shrugged as if I were supposed to have known he would make that ridiculous rule. I sighed, knowing that he was probably right. If there was something on the list that I didn't complete, it made little sense for it to be crossed off. But for the record, I never agreed.

I didn't want to jump out of an airplane. It wasn't my idea of fun. But, there was a small part of me—no matter how small that part may be—that argued it *was* my idea of living. Truly living. Pushing the limits . . . It terrified me. But there was a taste of something else too, something that I could only assume was excitement. What if I jumped and loved it? What if I thought it was exhilarating? Would I want to miss out on that? Of course not. And if I was going to be here as long as Easton had, or longer, shouldn't I know what I like? I guess I would have to jump to understand it. Understand me.

"OK. I'll do it," I said beneath my breath. Easton's face lit up. "But! We are amending that list!" I pointed my finger at him and raised a brow.

"Sure! I'll find a new menu, and we can make a new one!" Easton said. *Menu?* I wasn't sure what he meant about that. Not all of my memory had escaped the shadows, and some details I feared were lost forever. But after a year of asking for clarification, I grew sick of hearing myself question my first life. It only made me sad to think of the memories I had lost. Now, I only asked if I thought it might be important, and this didn't sound very important to me.

My stomach flipped about a hundred times before we even arrived at the headquarters. I'd been quiet during the training session, much like I was for the bungee jumping instruction. My mind a stew of nervous energy, regret, and a touch of nausea. Easton stepped away with his instructor. I watched nervously as he handed the guy cash and patted him on the back. I tried to focus, but my thoughts were scrambled.

"What was that?" I asked Easton upon his return.

"What?"

"That?" I motioned to where he stood with the instructor.

"Oh, just a tip. I figured I better tip him now so that we get the best experience."

"Did you tip my partner too?" I asked, looking between the instructors.

"Of course. It's for both of them," Easton said.

I thought about the tip and what it meant to have poor service from your skydiving instructor. This wasn't the kind of service you would expect from a restaurant. This was my life. And I was about to jump out of a plane thousands of feet in the sky. "You tipped them good, right?" I asked.

Easton chuckled, "I tipped them real good."

The full panic didn't set in until we loaded onto the plane. There was only room for four passengers, Easton and I fit snuggly with our certified instructors.

"This is a Cessna 182, small but mighty. It's the workhorse of skydiving planes," Easton's tandem partner said. A middle-aged man with a fit physique and a weathered face. "It will take us about twenty minutes to climb to 10,000 feet, and then we will jump."

"You have twenty minutes to get it together. Are you ready?" Easton said, leaning into my ear.

I swallowed the lump in my throat. Twenty minutes before I jumped out of a plane? Ready? *Never* . . . I shook my head. Easton grabbed my knee and squeezed it. His instructor went on about the plane's history, but as soon as the engine started, I no longer heard a word of it. My mind in another place completely. I sat still, my breathing shallow. Every now and again, my body would tremble. I knew I was afraid. Terrified even. But what exactly was that? Was it real? Make believe? Could I control it? Conquer it? I had no other choice but to figure it out because, in no time, my instructor stood and signaled for me to stand, too. I was really doing this thing.

I closed my eyes as my tandem partner secured us together. Strapped to my back was a professional. He had done this a thousand times over, and I had nothing to worry about. Nothing to think about. Nothing to do. I was merely along for the ride. Which turned out to be perfect, because my mind had frozen up again. I couldn't be trusted with the smallest of tasks now. Not even breathing.

Easton's instructor waved us ahead. I didn't want to go first, but there was no verbalizing that, or anything else, for that matter. It was far too late for any request. We stepped up to the plane's edge, and I lifted my head high, refusing to look down. The blood drained from my face as I turned to see Easton, his grin wide with excitement. He was handling this much better than when we went bungee jumping in Sin City. If I had only jumped that day, perhaps I would have found the excitement in this, too. I tried to swallow, but the saliva stuck in the back of my throat like tar. I wanted to tell Easton I loved him . . . just in case I didn't make it. But my mouth, along with everything else, was beyond my control, and I could no longer speak. I vaguely heard my instructor talking to me over the Cessna's hum, but I couldn't process what he said. My goggles were tight. Too tight. It was the last complete thought I had before I was pushed from behind.

My shoes scrapped against the platform as I was thrust forward. My stomach dropped, making me want to curl in on myself, and my eyes quickly found the ground that I had refused to look at. Realizing just how far up I was, I wanted to scream, but I had no breath. No voice. I closed my eyes tight. The fear encapsulating me. Suffocating me until I couldn't take it anymore. If there was such a thing as controlling the fear, I hadn't learned it. Far from it. And I'd be damned if I ever gave myself another chance to try.

The wind lashed against my cheeks and flushed through my mouth, hitting the back of my throat and drying it out. I opened my eyes and saw another sky diver flicker in my peripheral vision before quickly closing them again. The ground was so far it made me feel ill, and I couldn't think of anything worse than enduring the fear of falling to my death *and* puking all over my instructor. Though I wasn't convinced that I would live to feel the mortification of it, I still didn't want to die having it be one of the last thoughts in my mind.

My body trembled inside so fiercely my heart felt as if it

were vibrating. Some may call it exhilaration, but I was certain I was nothing but petrified. When the landing approached at lightning speeds, I felt the sensation of being pulled backward. It all happened so fast, and I hardly understood it until I bravely opened my eyes and the fall had slowed down, giving my mind a chance to comprehend it all.

I looked around frantically at the world below. More and more detail coming into vision as the earth approached. I looked around me, trying to find Easton, but all I could see was a neon orange and blue parachute flapping in the wind and one other jumper. I looked back to the ground, bracing myself for the land. When we touched down, I was useless. My legs were soft as Jell-O, and my eyes scrunched closed until I was positive I had survived. When I was detached from my instructor, I fell straight to my knees and gripped the grass in my hands.

"Wow! Are you OK?" my tandem asked. I nodded, catching my breath. He put his hand on my shoulder. "Are you going to be sick?" he asked.

"No," I said breathlessly. I willed myself to formulate a question, "Where is Easton?" I asked, looking up at him. My instructor stood, ignoring my question and nodded to the other jumper who had landed beside us.

"Hey, great jump!" the other guy said. I looked over at him, still on my knees like a fool. When he took his goggles off, I did the same, slowly recognizing him as Easton's tandem. My brows pulled tight as I surveyed the grounds. Easton wasn't anywhere in sight. What was going on?

"Where's Easton?" I asked again. This time louder and

more demanding. However, it came off as meek and breathless.

My instructor put his hands up, and my eyes shot to Easton's partner. His eyes grew large as he stalled, trying to find the words. "He . . . he's still with the Cessna," he said.

"He's what?" I hissed.

The men chuckled as they helped me to my feet. "Come on; you will see him back at the facility. He's going to meet us there."

"Wait, what?" I asked again, confused. I looked around, not seeing him anywhere. The realization crept into my head that I hadn't seen him in the air either. My jaw dropped open as the pieces fell into place. He hadn't jumped at all. "That . . . little shit," I said beneath my breath.

The men laughed. I heard one of them mutter, "I wouldn't want to be him in fifteen minutes."

My heart still fluttering and my legs still wobbly, I crawled into the van. We had a quick ride back to where we started our training and back to where I would find my cowardly husband. I had no idea what I would do to him when I found him, but I knew one thing. He was about to experience my full wrath. I sat in the van stewing while the men chatted amongst themselves. And when we arrived, I saw the plane parking outside of my window. I watched as Easton climbed out with a smug smile, and my heart rate picked up once more. I wondered where my relaxing vacation had gone.

Easton and I locked eyes from across the tarmac. A smile spread wide across his face, making me even angrier. I strode towards him. All the fears I had previously had turned to rage. How dare he make me jump . . . alone. "You!" I came at him with my finger pointed.

"Me?" Easton looked taken aback. His smile faded with every step closer I got.

"How could you? Just leave me up there, all by myself? You! You! You . . . *asshole!*" I fumed. The instructors were laughing in amusement.

"Wow, wow, wow." Easton held up his hands. "You do recall a certain bungee jumping incident where you begged me to jump with you? Right? And then, on the count of three, I was the only one propelling off the building? You do remember that, right?" Easton asked, eyes defensive.

I couldn't deny it. Not with the instructors present, and not when we had talked about it that very morning. "So!" I fumed.

"So?" Easton laughed. "So . . . you started it!" he said.

Anger boiled under my skin, and I channeled it all towards him. "You're going to pay for that little stunt you pulled, you know that?" I thrust my hand on my hip. My arms still like Jell-O as I tried to look tough. All three of the guys were laughing now, including Easton. It only made me more furious.

"Come on. . ." He said, reaching his hand out for me.

"No!" I jerked back, swatting his hand away. I did the only thing I could think of at the moment. "You're cut off!" I said.

All three of the guys stiffened. "Cut off?" Easton asked. One instructor looked to the other.

"From sex! How's that for a honeymoon?" I said.

The instructors howled with laughter, but Easton didn't find it so funny. "Wait . . ." He said, reaching for me as I turned to walk away. "Wait! Beck, wait a second!" he called out.

I marched on, crossing my arms and ignoring Easton. It may have been a more dramatic exit if I had somewhere to go or a car to take me away. Instead, I stood by the side of the building, waiting for the guys to catch up with me and tell me where to go. When they caught up, the instructors sat Easton and me down to see the video they had captured, both from a camera on my partner's wrist and one on the guy's helmet that captured the tandem jump. I crossed my arms as they loaded the video and explained the different movie packages they could turn the raw film into. I didn't need a video of me skydiving; I only needed to get out of this place and head back to my sanctuary. Maybe take a long walk on the beach. Alone.

"At least I was brave enough to jump!" I hissed under my breath.

"You were so brave, baby!" Easton tried to rub my shoulder, but I pulled away.

"I experienced it! And that's more than you can say!" I said.

"You're right."

"And it was just like flying. It was amazing, and I'm just mad because you didn't get to experience all the beauty with me," I lied.

"Really?" Easton asked, shocked. "And now you know you love it! Aren't you proud of yourself?" Easton asked.

"Yeah, I am! Are you?" I asked, in a snarky tone. I

wasn't proud of myself. Had I not been strapped to someone twice my size, they never would have gotten me out of that plane. I really had done nothing to be proud of at all, but fall ten thousand feet.

"Hey . . . It was just a joke. You can hang it over my head for as long as we live. Just like I'm going to do to you about the Sin City incident. But hey, you can cross it off your list now. Right?" Easton tried and tried to make it better.

"It wasn't even on my list!" I snapped. Crossing my arms tighter as I let it sink in. I had at least been able to say that I had skydived. And I guess that was pretty neat. I'd done it. I didn't like it, but I'd experienced it, nonetheless. And not many people could say as much. At least Easton couldn't. Not today, anyway.

The video started, and I recoiled at the sight of my face. I hadn't recognized myself. It wasn't a face I was used to seeing in the mirror—white as a ghost and fear stricken. My cheeks full of air like a chipmunk as they flapped in the wind. And then… and then something happened. I leaned forward in my seat, closer to the screen of the TV. Easton burst into laughter as my limp, lifeless body hung from my tandem partner's chest. I had passed out. And I hadn't even realized it.

My eyes flickered to the instructors, who stifled their laughter, but it was Easton who let it all out. He stomped the floor with his shoes and wrapped his arms around his waist. Right when I was about to say something malicious, I came to on the video making a moaning sound that reminded me of a cat in heat. I whipped my attention back to the screen and watched as my eyes rolled back into my head as I passed out again, and my face slackened. It happened again.

"Flying?" Easton asked. I gritted my teeth, fuming. I knew I hadn't flown through the sky, but I at least thought I could make it sound like Easton had missed out. Though after watching this video, this living proof, it was clear Easton had missed nothing but a display of my crippling fear. I turned to yell at Easton, but then I came to consciousness on the video, pulling my attention away once more. The terror would return to my face right before I would fall limp again. I'd never seen anything like it.

The embarrassment radiated off my back and heated to a boil. All this big talk about me having skydiving experience, and I hadn't experienced it at all. Unbeknownst to me, I essentially slept through the whole damn thing. I closed my eyes, wishing that I had just thrown up on my partner instead. It seemed like the lesser evil at the time, and by the way he was laughing at me, he deserved it.

There, in a small room with three guys rolling in hysterics, and my embarrassment about to burst into flames, I did the only thing I could. At first, it was a twitch of the lips. I tried to control it. I tried to hide it. I wanted to be furious! But every time I ran through another cycle of consciousness on the TV, I just about died all over again. It was the most ridiculous thing I had ever seen or experienced. And the idea of me not even knowing it was beyond me. A laugh broke loose, and my body jolted forward. I covered my mouth. But as soon as it was out, there was no going back. The guys laughed even louder now that they had full permission, and I covered my watering eyes with my hands, unable to control my rollercoaster of emotions.

My feet were safely planted on the ground, and I had survived a 10,000-foot jump. And I suppose, whether or not I passed out, I could still say that I did it. And the fact that it was so incredibly embarrassing . . . well, that just made for a better story, I guess.

"Yes! We'll take it! We'll take the best video package you offer!" Easton barked between fits of laughter.

"No!" I wailed, jumping to my feet.

CHAPTER 11

lames twirled between the dancers and over their heads. Their hips knocked side to side with a speed I couldn't possibly comprehend. Their banana leaf sarongs left little to the imagination, but that hadn't stopped me. I couldn't dance like that if I had decades of training. It made me wonder what it felt like to perform a fire dance, but I ultimately concluded that it was just a job for them. An everyday mundane task. Their Monday, and my entertainment. It hardly seemed fair, and I wished they enjoyed it the way I did now. Who knew? Maybe they did?

"Does this ever get old?" I asked Easton across the table. I didn't take my eyes off the dancers, and I wasn't sure that he'd heard me, or even if I had said it aloud. If I truly had lives upon lives to live, would this ever get old? Would something so amazing as raw talent become boring at some point? Had it been boring for Easton now?

"What?" Easton replied, reaching across the table to take my hand.

"This."

"The nearly naked men?"

"No! The show! The talent . . . the extraordinary talent. Does it all become, I don't know, *ordinary* after a while? After seeing it so many times in so many lives, does it lose what makes it special?" I asked, and only then did I pull my eyes from the fire dancers to look at Easton. The glow of the fire waltzed across his face in the dark of the night. I didn't want to hear his answer.

Easton looked from me to the dancers, thinking about my question, and I could only imagine that he was trying to come up with something positive to say. But the truth was probably anything but. It was old news to him. I don't know why I thought it wasn't, but it still hurt a bit. I didn't want to live forever if I'd be stuck in an endless loop of been there's or done that's. I could see how it would be considered a curse.

"This show doesn't really do much for me. Maybe because I've seen it a time or two before. Maybe because there are men in banana leaves . . ." Easton shrugged. I smiled and briefly scanned the beach for the women in coconuts that were surely going to dance next. "But it hasn't lost its charm. And being here with you makes it almost new again. Being with you is like getting to see it for the first time. I get to see the wonder in your eyes, and honestly, it's probably the most I've ever enjoyed it, which is saying a lot."

"Are you just saying that?" I asked, looking him square in the eyes.

"No, I'm not," he said.

"I used to be afraid of dying. Of not experiencing life. Of not having enough time. And now that I have the opportunity to do it all, I'm just as afraid. But for different reasons." I sighed, and Easton tightened his grip on my hand. "Now I'm afraid of becoming callused. I'm worried that I'll turn numb to all the beautiful things around me. I just feel so at peace here, on the island. And the thought of coming back one day and not feeling this way because I've seen it so many times is just . . . it's just sad," I said. "I don't want it to happen."

"Beck, do you think you could ever, truly, tire of this?"

I looked around. The fire dancers were bowing, and the small dinner crowd applauding. I clapped and watched them walk away. Their tan buns covered by one single leaf. "God, I hope not!" I said. Easton laughed, and before I knew it, a dinner roll hit my chest. I jumped and caught it before it rolled off my chair. "Hey! I'm just saying!"

"I'm just saying… I don't think you have anything to worry about," Easton said, with a twinkle in his eye.

I smiled, placing the dinner roll back on the table. Maybe I was overthinking it. Maybe my predisposition was to worry, no matter what. I would always find something new to fear. I was always going to be my own worst enemy.

A server approached our table, filling our water and giving us a clean plate for the buffet dinner. Easton and I walked to the back of the line that comprised of three honeymoon couples. All young, though we must have had them beat by at least five years. Easton began loading up his plate, and I passed on the smoked pork and macadamia nut crusted sea bass. By the time we walked back to our table, my plate had only gained a single scoop of white rice and a small chicken thigh. And that didn't even appeal to me, but I insisted on getting something on my plate, and it was one of my last options.

"Is that all your eating?" Easton asked, holding a full dinner plate of his own.

I looked down at my pathetic chicken and rice. "I'm just not that hungry," I said with a shrug.

"OK. Well, we can go somewhere else if you want?"

"No, it's not that. I'm honestly just not hungry." I picked up my fork and pushed my rice around on my plate. And when I felt Easton's eyes grow with worry, I forced myself to eat the chicken.

"Are you still mad at me about the skydiving? Is that what this is?" Easton asked.

I looked at him sideways. "Do you honestly think I would starve myself because I was mad at you? What would that accomplish?" I asked.

Easton nodded. "Good point."

"And yes. I am still mad at you," I added.

"Oh? How long is that going to last?" Easton asked. As if it were that simple. We had fought before, sure, but we had never been in a situation where time wasn't fleeting, or the urgency of past memories wasn't creeping out of the shadows and demanding answers. No, we had all the time in the world, and I knew who and what I was. I could simply hold this grudge forever . . . or not, I hadn't decided. "I don't know yet."

"Why don't you show me how mad you are tonight?" Easton's brow rose.

"Nope. You're cut off, remember." I shrugged, looking away just as the women in coconut shells took center stage. Easton looked at them, frowning, and I couldn't help but giggle. "How's that for charm?" I asked. His eyes blazed back to me with a deep burning lust lit from within. I swallowed down a lump in my throat, determined to make him pay for not jumping with me earlier in the day. "No," I said. My mouth suddenly dry.

"No, what?" he asked.

"No. I said no." I looked away, feeling his eyes burrow into me. For the life of me, I couldn't figure out why a smile spread across my lips, but for some reason, I was simply amused. His yearning for me. Me pretending to be strong. Because that's all it was . . . make believe. Just because I was mad at him didn't make me want him any less. He just didn't need to know that part.

Easton finished his dinner, and we ducked out early. The dancers had endless moves, and the show would continue for some time. But there was something romantic about sneaking away while most of the resort guests sat hypnotized by the flames thrown into the sky. Easton pulled my hand, and we ran across the rock paths covered by lush green archways and bountiful flowers. The further we fled from the dinner show, the quieter it became. And when the drums were a distant beat, Easton laid his lips on mine.

He ran his hand up the nape of my neck, deepening the kiss. I all but forgot about what I had said to him back on the tarmac. His hands ran the length of my side before he pulled away, lowering his forehead to mine and taking in a breath. "Let's go back to our room," he suggested huskily. I didn't need convincing. We took off, heading straight for our bungalow. And though the walk was long, the tension built with time. And when we made it back to our room, we had all but collapsed on the bed doing what lovers do best.

My head swam, and the room spun as I worked to catch my breath. My skin was covered in a thin sheen of sweat. "God, you're right!" I grabbed my temples as the spinning slowed, and the room became still once again.

"Always. But what about this time?" Easton asked, panting.

I rolled onto my side and stared up at him as he lay on his back. His hair disheveled like he had been caught in a wind storm. Easton lifted his hand and brushed the hair off my cheek, tucking it behind my ear. "I don't think this life could ever lose its magic," I said.

Easton smiled at me for a sweet but fleeting moment. Before I knew it, I had been swept up in his arms, and he was running straight for our patio. "Easton, no!" I screamed, clenching my arms around his neck. "No!" I wailed as he lept right off our dock, baring less than the fire dancers. The ocean splashed as we plummeted under water, and for a moment, the fear inside me seized up.

I remembered most of my last life, though it had been blurry and the details lacking. But the one memory I relived all the time clearer than the day itself was the accident in which we drowned. I relived it in my sleep, in the shower, and most of all, I relived it when I was near large bodies of water. And plunging into the black ocean was a definite trigger. I fought fiercely, pushing Easton down and climbing up his back like a ladder to my survival. I breached the surface and gasped for air, hungry for the first time that night. I splashed about erratically.

"Hey, hey!" Easton took ahold of me and swam to the ladder. I clung on for dear life. "Are you OK? What was that?" he asked, panting nearly as much as me.

Feeling safer with the ladder in hand, I felt utterly stupid for the way I'd reacted. I nodded, focusing on the moon glistening over the dancing ripples of the water's surface and tried to slow my breath. My instincts told me to get out of the water. Climb the ladder. Get on the dock. But I did no such thing. My legs kicked slowly as my heartbeat slowed. The water was warmer than I imagined it would be, and it felt weird against my skin without a swimsuit on. A tiny part of me almost enjoyed the freedom.

"Come to me," Easton said, floating a couple of feet away. I wanted to, but I wasn't ready to let go of the ladder. "Nobody can see us," he said.

"It's not that." I searched the other bungalows for signs of life, anyway.

"Is it the accident?" Easton asked softly.

I didn't have to answer. My silence confirmed it all. "Trust me," he said, holding out a hand. I did. I trusted him. Not to jump out of a plane with me . . . But I trusted him with my heart and certainly with my safety. I placed my hand in his, and he pulled me to him. The warm water brushed past my bare body. "Turn around and float onto your back," he said.

"I can't. I don't float."

"Just take deep breaths. Fill your lungs and be still. I'll

do the rest." Easton pulled on the nape of my neck, holding my face out of the water. My body rose to the surface, and I startled, kicking my legs and arms about. "Shhh. Just relax." I did everything I could to do just that. I took the deep breaths, and I noticed that my body would sink a little when I exhaled. But with every inhale, it would rise again. After some time, I trusted that I wouldn't sink to the ocean floor and history would not repeat itself. Eventually, I closed my eyes, and without my knowledge, Easton had let go. I felt free. Free of the trauma from drowning in the river and free of my worries of the future. The gentle rise and fall of my breath like a life raft in the moonlit ocean. I had been floating all by myself, and all I ever needed was the support of Easton to help me trust myself.

Of course, it all came crashing down the second I opened my eyes to find him several feet away. But until that moment—when he had to help me back to the dock, and I tried to drown him all over again—it was nothing short of magic. It would be a moment I'd look back upon. An example of the many times in my life that I was too afraid to do something I could fully do all on my own.

After my first real dip in the ocean ended, my stomach knotted with what I assumed was hunger for skipping most of my dinner. I placed my hand on my stomach, frowning. "I think I'm going to run to the gift shop and get a snack," I said, toweling off.

"Finally getting hungry?" Easton said as he ran the towel through his hair.

"Yeah."

"Want me to come with you?" he asked.

"No, that's OK. I won't be long," I said, needing time to quiet my mind. Time to feel the water in my lungs and trust that I'm OK now. That *I am OK*. I slipped on my flip-flops and turned to smile at Easton before leaving.

"Hey, Beck?" he said.

"Yeah?"

"We can cross skinny dipping off your list." Easton winked at me, and my smile grew. I hadn't recalled the details of the list he spoke of, but it didn't surprise me that skinny dipping was on it since I made the list pre-drowning. I took in a deep breath as I strolled down the dock. The ocean's sultry brine in the air and the lapping of the water . . . I didn't know if it would be enough three hundred years from now, but I knew Easton would be.

I opened the gift shop door and walked inside. Tiny goosebumps covered my arms as soon as the air conditioning hit my skin, and I rubbed my arms as I walked the isles. Nothing looked appetizing, but I settled on salty crackers and a ginger ale. As I waited in line behind a mother and her daughter, I couldn't help but stare at the chubby curly-haired toddler. "Dis one?" she asked in a high-pitched tone.

"Not that one," the mother said.

"Dis one?" The girl asked for a new candy bar.

"Not that one. . ."

"Dis one?" Each time she asked with the same renewed enthusiasm, and I couldn't help but smile. The excitement in her eyes over each possible candy bar was nearly too much to handle, and I felt a flood of emotion crash into me like a rogue wave. A burn hit the back of my throat, and I wondered what had possibly come over me. The mother and daughter finished checking out, and the little girl never got her candy bar. She screamed as the mom carried her out. I frowned.

"Hello. Is this all for you tonight?" the store clerk asked when I put my crackers and drink on the table.

Had I been emotional over the wreckage? Was it that I had just taken a step in overcoming my fear of drowning? Or was it something even bigger than that? Had I been afraid my life would grow dull without the one thing in this world I knew I couldn't have? I looked back to the clerk and then to the display behind her.

"Um, just one more thing," I said, listening to the girl's cry fade away.

"$22.99, please," the clerk said.

I took out my cash and paid. As I waited for my receipt, I looked back to the glass door and beyond into the night. The little girl was gone, and her cries all but distant. And at that moment, I had to wonder if my emotion came from the fear of never having a little girl of my own. Would my life be enough without it?

CHAPTER 12

The following day was a day of rest. Easton and I lounged on our dock for most of it as I didn't feel well. I should have felt more relaxed as time slipped by, but I felt worse. My stomach hadn't been the same since the buffet, and the crackers I bought at the gift shop did little to settle it. Today was our last full day on the island, and I was determined to make the best of it. My stomach churned, and my mouth watered upon rising in the morning, but I laced my shoes, anyway. I wouldn't miss the waterfall if it were the last thing I did.

When I caught a glance at my reflection in the mirror, I looked peckish. I took a couple of deep breaths through my mouth before dusting on some blush and bronzer. I didn't want Easton to know that I was still ill. It was our honeymoon and the tail end of it, too. I wasn't going to ruin any bit of it for either of us. I didn't want to look back on this memorable trip three hundred years from now and wish I'd just sucked it up for the last day. A little indigestion would not slow me down. *Indigestion* . . . I kept calling it that.

I packed a light backpack alongside Easton as we prepped for our hike to the Wabo Waterfall. It was the most beautiful waterfall on Taiseen Island and well known around the world. We would need to get a ride to the trailhead. Then it would be five miles up and five miles back. It should be easy enough. However, with the humidity and my newfound sensitive stomach, I was expecting a moderate to difficult hike ahead.

"Are you bringing your trunks?" I asked as I shoved leftover crackers in my backpack. Easton motioned to his lower half. He was already wearing them. Black and blue stripes with a white drawstring. He had purchased them here on the island the day we arrived. "Right," I said.

"Are you alright? You seem a little off?" Easton asked.

"I'm good. Just a little tired. Who knew vacationing could be so exhausting, right?" I smiled, and Easton wagged his brows, making me roll my eyes in response. I guess we hadn't exactly taken it easy on the extracurricular activities. My cheeks heated.

"How's your stomach today?" Easton asked, zipping up his bag.

"It's great!" I said, hiding my pale face under makeup. He'd never know.

"Yeah? Do you have your appetite back?"

"Mmm...Yup!" My voice squeaked under the pressure of the lie.

Easton sighed, "Oh good! I was beginning to think your cancer was returning or . . ." Easton stiffened as soon as it slipped from his mouth. Regret washed over his face as his brows pulled in. He avoided meeting my eye.

"No. Never. Just some funky island chicken or something," I said. I had remembered little about my cancer, and it was one topic I liked to stay away from. I had many unanswered questions, but I never dared to ask about them. Was I sad? Was my family heartbroken? Probably. I didn't see how recalling such a difficult time in one of my lives would help me now. Burying the whole thing in the black void of my subconscious was most likely the best place for such memories. And for now, I was content with that. They could sit there for decades . . . centuries . . . Collecting dust for all I cared. As long as they didn't come out from the shadows, I was a strong and capable new me.

"You think you ate that chicken that was walking in circles on the beach the other day?" Easton asked.

I laughed, "That's the one! I know it."

Easton called for a ride to the mouth of the Wabo Waterfall Trail, and we waited in front of the resort for what seemed like a small eternity. Everything moved slowly on the island, and I both appreciated it and was driven mad by the same thing. Today though, I was driven mad. Maybe it was the muggy warm island air, or the sweat cultivating on my back and in between my chest . . . or maybe it was the slow churn of my stomach that made me impatient. Either way, I convinced myself that it would all be better as soon as I could sit in the air conditioning of the cab and rest for just a few minutes before our hike began. I tapped my foot with anticipation.

When the cab pulled up, I had my doubts about feeling

better. And when I tossed my backpack inside the old car and crawled in after it, I knew. The cab was like a sauna, and air conditioning was a luxury this little thing could not afford. I swallowed and took a deep breath. Both sweat and cigarette smoke marinated inside the cab and wafted in the air. My mouth watered again. I rolled down my window, crank by crank, and leaned into the muggy air, startling when the cab went over its first twig in the road. Apparently, suspension was also a luxury. Easton took my hand lovingly, and I could tell without looking at him that he was worried. I forced myself to hold his hand, even though it made my whole body feel ten degrees hotter than before.

By the time we got to the trailhead, I all but tumbled out of the car. Opening my door before the car was fully parked, I lurched out of the sweat-infused sauna. I'd been working really hard to keep myself together, but I couldn't do it any longer. I vomited small amounts of stomach acid on the side of the road. And when I was done, to my surprise, the nausea remained. It hadn't eased one bit. I closed my eyes with disappointment in myself. I tried so hard not to ruin the day.

"Are you OK?" Easton asked, rubbing my back.

"Yup. I'm good. That was just the smell. You know. The cab," I said, refusing to look at him. I pointed my finger aimlessly down the road toward the car as it drove away, a cloud of dust in its wake.

"Hey, why don't we just go back to the resort, and you can lie down? Maybe watch a movie or take a nap?"

"No," I whined.

"Beck?" Easton started.

"Please? Easton, I really want to see the waterfall. I don't feel . . . *steller*, but, I believe I can do it . . ."

"You . . . *believe*?" Easton's eyes lasered in on mine, forcing me to look away.

I sighed. "I *can* do it. Come on!" I didn't give him a choice. I wiped my mouth on my arm and took off down the trail, never looking back.

"Beck!" Easton called out. I shook my head in refusal and kept walking. The gravel crunching under my shoes. "Beck!" Easton called out.

"Nope!" I kept walking.

"Beck! It's this way!"

"Damn it!" I hissed, slowing my stubborn pace just long enough to shake off the embarrassment before spinning on my heels and walking back to Easton and the forked trail. Unfortunately, I made the mistake of peeking at him as I passed by. His lips pulled up at the corners as our eyes met. The smirk on his face only made me furious.

My aggravated pace didn't last long, and before I knew it, I needed a break. I kneeled over to retie my shoes, not wanting to look weak. I was able to catch my breath just a little, but it wasn't enough. Shortly thereafter, I officially announced it was break time. We must have only been a mile into the trail, but I was hot and breathless. I cursed the chicken who walked in circles on the beach. And every time a little voice in my head told me it wasn't the chicken, my mouth would run, silencing my mind. I would say anything if it meant I didn't have to hear myself think.

"Think there are geckos out here?" I blurted out.

"Um, yeah. Probably."

"Boas! What about them?" I looked up at the trees, waiting for a long vine to slink through the branches.

"Uh, I don't know. But I don't think you need to worry about that."

I nodded. Opening my backpack to take out my water. I riffled through my bag, and my eye caught on the pregnancy test I had bought at the gift shop two nights ago. "Spider Monkeys! For sure though . . . Right?" I zipped up my backpack without ever taking my water out.

"No. Definitely not. Hey, are you OK?" Easton asked again.

I wasn't OK. I was sick, I was worried, and worse yet, maybe even a little excited. Which, in all honesty, only worried me more. "Yeah. Let's go!" I threw my backpack over my shoulder and jumped to my feet. Easton followed cautiously behind me. What if I actually was excited at the possibility of being pregnant but then found out not only that I wasn't, but that I never would be? What if I was pregnant but wasn't ready? What if Easton wasn't ready?

I didn't take the test yesterday because I was sure I wasn't pregnant. After all, Easton was sterile. He was over three hundred years old for crying out loud. It was impossible. And the only reason I was sick was because of the crazy chicken . . . The one I know was not served that night for dinner. I took a deep breath and admitted to myself that I had seen that very chicken doing donuts in the sand the following day.

"I can't wait to see that waterfall!" I blurted out once more. I was beginning to feel like a crazy person. My physical voice silencing my mental one. They were both fighting for my attention, and neither one of them was winning. At some point, I had to believe that taking the test and finding out that I wasn't pregnant was far better than this slow torture I was putting myself through. I was stressing myself out for no reason at all.

"Do you hear it?" Easton asked.

"Hu?" *Was he talking?*

"Do you hear the waterfall?" I turned back to look at Easton, and his expression was all I needed to help pull me back to the present. And there it was, the deep rumbling calls from a grand waterfall. "We're close!" Easton said. I forced a smile and searched the distant trail for signs of the famous Wabo Waterfall. The sound grew louder with each step, and my gait quickened in anticipation of the beauty that hid just up the trail. My mind snapped back like a rubber band that had stretched too far. *I should just take it. Now. Like right now!* "No!" I said out loud.

"What's that?" Easton asked.

"Talk to me? Tell me something. A story?" I asked, needing the distraction because the lush green scenery was no longer doing it for me. And neither was the fear of an enormous boa constrictor dropping from the trees.

"Um . . . OK, so this one time, during World War I." Easton sighed deeply, taking a moment to gather his thoughts. "It was twenty-four hours before the bullet pierced my chest, and perhaps the craziest twenty-four hours of my lives. It started at twilight during the battle—"

"I have to pee!" I called out, darting off trail and stomping over large spikey bushes till I found one that was large enough to squat behind. I was determined to put my mind to ease. This whole thing was ridiculous. I unzipped my backpack and pulled out the pregnancy test. I clawed the box open and pulled the cap off the stick. Grasping the test tight in my hand, I pulled my pants down and squatted behind the bush. Getting pee all over my ankles and hand, I was sure that I had at least gotten something on the stick itself. My breath quickened as I pulled my pants back on. I returned the clear cap and stared at the window for my future to unveil itself.

CHAPTER 13

My eyes glued to the little window on the pregnancy test. I wasn't sure if I was seeing things or not. I blinked several times to moisten my dry eyes and ensure I was seeing it clearly.

"Are you OK, Beck? Did you see one of those spider monkeys?" Easton called from the trail.

My face heated, but I said nothing in return. The window started to change. A faint blue began to appear in a thin line across the screen. The second I saw it, I stashed the test deep within my backpack and zipped it up, locking my future inside. Unseen. Unknown.

Popping to my feet, I yelled out, "Coming!" I must have been as white as a ghost by the time I got back to the trail, and by the disapproving look Easton gave me, I gathered I might have looked even worse than I originally thought. I didn't know what blue meant on the test, but I did know that blue universally represented boys and pink was for girls. Was I having a baby boy? I cursed myself for clawing open the box without reading the instructions. Here I had convinced myself it couldn't be any worse than the ongoing battle in my head, and yet I had found a way to make it worse. Much worse. Now I had my answer, and I didn't know what it meant.

Did I even want to have a baby? A boy? I was only twenty-two, barely old enough to take care of myself. How was I going to take care of a baby? And what were people going to think? That I got married so young because I was pregnant? Nice. Nice, I thought. I was so wrapped up in my thoughts I didn't realize the five-mile hike to the Wabo Waterfall was complete. The waterfall, bold and beautiful, gushed before me, and in that moment, I couldn't understand what it meant when my hand reached for my belly. I let it linger there for just a little while before I took in the view. The nausea had broken, and I felt at peace.

"Wow, look at that? Have you ever seen anything so beautiful?" I asked. Easton stood by my side, watching me. "Every day," he said. It was so ridiculous to think that I could compete with this world-renowned wonder, but I blushed anyway. Easton leaned over and kissed me softly on the lips. His glacier eyes so accepting. I didn't know why I felt the need to carry this burden all on my own. I knew I didn't have to. "Let's sit over there on that rock. Are you hungry yet? I brought snacks," he said.

I nodded. Not in a way that was a lie, but more of an encouragement. Easton helped me crawl on top of a large boulder, and though it was uncomfortable to sit on, the view was stunning. I pulled my backpack onto my lap while Easton situated himself. Droplets of the waterfall spat at us, and every now and again, it would startle me. "You know I had this dream. A nightmare, really. It haunted me for months when I was looking for you. There were these twin boulders, just like this." Easton slapped the rock. "I was so convinced they would crush me."

"What happened?" I asked.

"They didn't."

"Huh. . ." I watched Easton examine the boulder. It didn't seem much of a dream to me, be he seemed fascinated.

"So, is it everything you hoped it would be?" Easton asked as he laid out a few snacks in front of us.

"It's more. I feel like it's calming all my worries. I just feel at peace here," I said in wonder.

"All your worries? What's wrong?"

"Oh, just, you know. Feeling sick and what not." I opened my backpack slowly and carefully. I pulled out my water and crackers. But not before I took another peek at the pregnancy test results. I was shocked to see it now had two blue lines. I pretended to be looking for something as I grabbed the ripped box and tried to piece the directions together. Maybe it was the pressure of Easton sitting right next to me, or maybe it was the dim lighting within my backpack, but I couldn't tell what I was looking at.

"What did you forget?" Easton peered into my backpack. I snapped the bag shut, causing suspicion to rise in his eyes.

"Nothing!"

"Beck?"

"Nothing!"

"Beck, come on." Easton reached over for my bag, and I pulled it away instinctively. I knew all too well I was only making him more suspicious, but I couldn't help it. It was pure instinct. "What is going on?" he asked when the weird turned to uncomfortable.

"I flushed your wedding band down the toilet!" I blurted out.

"What?" Alarm sounded in Easton's voice as I closed my eyes and tilted my head up toward the mouth of the Wabo Waterfall. I didn't want to know what his face looked like. "You what?" He exclaimed, his voice even higher now. I sucked in a slow, quivering breath. His accusation began, "You told me that—"

"I'm pregnant!" I blurted out.

The humid air grew so thick it was hard to breathe. And the silence grew louder with every passing second. I opened my eyes, but I didn't look at him. I stood up on the boulder and placed my hands on my hips, staring out at countless gallons of water that poured over the steep rocks. Once again, it did something to help ground me. Somehow, calm me. Telling me it would all be OK. How could it not, when something so beautiful as this existed?

After what seemed like a small eternity, Easton stood up and wrapped his arms around me, pulling me into his embrace. I didn't just become unglued, I broke. All the fear of uncertainty poured out of me like the Wabo Waterfall. I cried for a long time—long enough that my legs grew tired of standing, and my eyes had swelled. Easton held me tight through and through. I was thankful for the silence then because after my emotions poured out of me, my mind had finally quieted, and it was nice for a change.

"Are you sure?" Easton asked softly after we sat back down on the boulder. Was I *sure*? The terrible realization came over me that I wasn't *sure*. I was anything but *sure*. In actuality, the only thing I was *sure* of was that I had no clue how to read the instructions.

"Well, I took a test. . ." I said. Then I slowly unzipped my backpack and pulled it out, handing it to him.

Easton's brows furrowed, and he flipped the test over, examining it. "What does that mean?" he asked.

"Um. Boy?" I said, rubbing the back of my neck.

"Boy?" Easton glared at me, and I nodded. "I don't know much about pregnancy tests since I've never taken one, but I know that they don't tell you the gender of the baby." I swallowed the lump in my throat, holding his gaze bravely. "Do you have the instructions?"

"Yes!" I pulled the ripped box out of my backpack and handed it to Easton in pieces. He stared at me until I was uncomfortable enough I had to look away. I knew I had dropped the ball on this one. And while I can honestly say that the wedding band down the toilet was a whole-hearted mistake, this time, I just let my emotions get the better of me. I had to work on that. Staying calm under pressure and all. Gathering all the facts. And perhaps—not telling my husband I was pregnant before I really knew for *sure*—was something I should work on too. Lucky for me, I had all the time in the world to become perfect. I'd put that on my to do list.

"Beck. This is in French." Easton shook his head.

"Cut me some slack! I'm only on my second life here!" I belted out. We stared at each other, his glacier eyes against my emerald ones until he cracked. His smile made me giggle, and my giggle made him laugh. Before we knew it, I was crying all over again. Though for a different reason this time. This time, I felt foolish getting worked up over nothing. But what I hadn't realized before, was that I wasn't alone. I had Easton, and he was a pretty damn good companion to have by my side. That's why I married him after all.

"OK, so I knew French at one time. Bare with me, I'm a little rusty, but I'll do the best I can," he said.

"I thought you were a doctor?" I teased.

"I wasn't an O.B., Beck. And even if I were, we wouldn't have given our patients French urine tests. Blood tests are way more accurate than this hunk of plastic, OK?"

I shrugged. "Whatever you say, doctor," I said, leaving him to it. Easton matched the three pieces of the torn box together and tried to recall his French. He looked at the test several times, perhaps in disbelief. Eventually, he handed everything back to me. "Well, what did it say?" I asked.

"It says you're pregnant."

"It what?" I asked.

"It says your pregnant, but we will have to get a blood test when we get back." Easton shook his head.

"What? Why do you look like that?" I asked. Easton's eyes crinkled with worry.

"I don't think it's accurate, Beck. I don't want you to get your hopes up."

"Wait, why don't you think it's accurate?" Disappointment washed over me. I knew my hopes were already on the rise. I wanted to have a baby. And that was something that I'd never given thought to before now. Knowing it as clear as day wasn't something I could take back.

"I think I may have told you this before, but I can't have kids. I'm tethered. You are tethered. There's no way it can happen."

"But what if being a Tethered Soul is like being your own species? What if you just needed to find another Tethered Soul to make it work?" I asked. My voice whiney, like I was pleading for this to all make sense. It scared me to think how I might react to finding out I wasn't pregnant. And now that I knew I wanted this, what would it do to me to live for an eternity without ever having children? Being a Tethered Soul would surely be a curse then.

"I've never thought of it like that. I mean, I guess it's possible?" Easton questioned.

"Yeah." I nodded, not wanting to give up hope.

"But if that's the case, then the baby would be tethered too. And I don't want to do that to another soul," Easton said.

"Well, you did it to me!" I said.

"I did nothing to you. You followed me back here."

"Is that what I did? I just followed you here?" I waved my hand through the air.

"Look, I don't know what happened, I—"

"That's right! You don't know. So, let's not pretend we know the baby will be tethered because we don't. Fair?" I asked.

It took a moment, but Easton agreed. "Fair." He nodded, and I was a little taken aback by my hostile reaction. The words *mama bear* came to mind. I had to be pregnant. Why else would I be so protective over nothing? "It just hurts me to think that I could bring a baby into this world, and I could only protect it for one lifetime. Then, he would always be on his own. Fighting for himself, fighting to get back to us. I don't want that for him, and I don't want it for you. I would never have chosen this life for you." Easton's eyes glossed over, and I could see the reflection of the waterfall in them. The thought of not being able to protect a child was unbearable.

"I know you want to protect me. I get that, but I'm not so sure this thing is a curse, Easton. I'm just not convinced of that yet," I said.

"That's because you didn't remember for the first twenty-two years, and you had wonderful parents to make you feel loved. That doesn't happen every time. And when you wake up as a young child, and all of your memories come crashing down on you, and you realize it's not a dream any longer . . . that's when it becomes a curse. That's when you realize you're lost, and alone, and you can't find your way back home . . . Because you don't have one." Easton's voice was soft and full of pain.

His words hurt deep in my chest, and I felt for him and our unborn baby. Easton raked his hands through his hair, and it toppled back down in front of his face. "Don't you think we could be that home for him?" I asked. Worry lined my forehead, and I was pleading again. "Every year, we meet at the bridge. May seventh. Rain or shine; we reunite there. And we will be his home." It wasn't a question or a plea now, but a promise.

CHAPTER 14

The following day was a full day of travel. And even though I was nauseous again, I was happy because that meant that I may still be pregnant. I started calling it morning sickness, even though it lasted until well after lunch. The first thing I did when we finally got home was call an OB-GYN and make an appointment. The blood test was scheduled for the following week, and I could hardly wait. I slept like a rock that first night after returning home, and I blamed it on jetlag, but I knew better. I was exhausted from creating a human being. Still, there was a part of me—no matter how small it may be, that was a little superstitious—so I didn't admit it aloud.

The following day, after my sickness had subsided, I ventured to the park by my old house. It was something that I had been doing for the past year. Ever since Easton and I broke into my first parent's house. Sometimes I would sit there and read for a couple of hours. And sometimes, I would see Chloe and my nephew. He was young, maybe four or five, and I imagine she had him unexpectedly. Wes was much younger than my niece, Everly. Rarely, she would show up with Wes in tow. It was easier when she brought him; I never had to worry about being caught. But with Chloe, I did. I wore my spy gear, of course. The large sunglasses and hat. I pulled my hair back too and hid my face behind a good book. Many trips to the park, they would never show, and I would get some valuable reading time in.

Though today, on this sunny afternoon, Chloe and Wes did show. I hid my smiles behind my romance novel and my curious stares behind my mirrored lenses. She never had a second thought about the stranger that often sat on the bench, or if she did, she didn't show it.

Chloe glanced in my direction, giving me a polite wave, and I smiled, raising my book. Keep calm. She's done this a time or two before, she's just being nice. I lowered the book a mere inch at a time and was relieved when she hadn't closed the distance between us. I smiled again when I thought about how mad Easton would be if he found out I was here, playing with fire.

"Ma, who's that?" Wes asked, pointing to me. I was the only other person in the park. My insides twisted, and I squirmed a little in my seat.

"That's a lady."

"What's she doin?"

"She's reading."

"Why?"

"Because she wants to."

"Why?"

"Because it must be a good book."

"Why?"

"Do you want to go on the swings?"

"Yeah!"

I let out the breath I didn't know I had been holding when Wes gave up pursuing me. My heart pounded in my chest. It was closer than they had ever come to talking to me. I raised my book to cover my sunglasses and tried to read the first sentence in chapter seven. I must have read that first line a dozen times, and each time, it made no more sense than the first.

Was I really going to have a baby boy? Would he look like my nephew, Wes? Sandy hair and chubby cheeks. Would he be tethered? And if so, was that really all that bad? I didn't think being a Tethered Soul was a genetic disorder. After all, I only became tethered after falling for Easton. Or so I thought. Perhaps I had been tethered all along? Was that even possible? Had I had lives before that I simply didn't remember? I quickly dismissed the thought. It was far too disturbing. However, if being tethered was not a genetic anomaly, then my theory on being a different species and the whole reason Easton and I could get pregnant in the first place would be blown out of the water. In which case, I didn't know what to think.

The sun beat down on the nape of my neck, but I didn't dare let my hair down. I didn't want to give Chloe another reason to recognize me. I stared at the first line in my book while listening to his soft squeals on the swing. Chloe looked tired today. Maybe even a little sad. She had matured a lot in the last twenty-two years. Not just her clothing or lipstick, but her demeanor. Maybe it was the children that wore her down, but she seemed . . . calm. I worried it might be something else, but always faltered back to age. She must have just settled into her stride. Stopped worrying so much about what other people thought of her. I, for one, never liked her more.

Chloe was a good mom. I had only seen my brother once in my second life, and that was at my dad's funeral, but even then, he looked better than ever. He and Chloe appeared to be strong and happy. As happy as any could be under the circumstances. And I loved her for that. For taking care of my brother the way she has all these years. The fear that she wouldn't was the only reason I had such distastes for her in my first life. I was worried she wasn't good enough for him. Though now, I can see I was wrong. And I couldn't be more grateful. Sometimes while I sat at the park, I wondered if we would have been friends. But as I sat on the bench today, I knew we would be.

A green ball rolled to my feet, startling me from my thoughts. The quick pitter-patter of the little boy running through the grass grew louder as he approached me. Before I knew it, Wes was at my feet, picking up his ball. But he didn't pick it up and run—no—he picked it up and stared at me blankly. My stomach dropped as I slowly lowered my book. Chloe stood on the other side of the playground, watching, waiting.

But when Wes didn't move, and he didn't speak, I did something reckless. I lifted my sunglasses, and I winked at him. He stood stunned for a second, then took off running back to his mom. He pointed at me, repeating himself over and over again. "That's my siser! That's my siser!"

"That's not your sister, baby. That's just a woman at the park. She's reading." Chloe tried to calm him down. She swooped him up in her arms, but he craned his neck, trying to look at me still.

"That's my siser!" he yelled.

"OK. Time to go home, buddy. Come on, let's get your ball." Chloe packed her bag with one hand as she cradled Wes on her hip. She turned around right before leaving the park to look at me one last time. I dipped my head ever so slightly behind my book, regretting my decision to show myself to the boy. I had no idea he would be such a little snitch. Figures, I thought. He's my brother's son.

Chloe started for her car, but I could hear Wes calling louder and louder down the trail. Clearly upset that his mom wasn't listening to him. "That's my siser! That's Everee!"

My stomach sank when I heard my name escape his mouth. What had I done? It was clear that my niece and I looked similar, but how was I supposed to know he would solve the puzzle in a minute flat? Especially when I had been going to the park for an entire year now, and Chloe hadn't figured it out. I shook my head, feeling so stupid. The only reason Wes knew it was me when Chloe hadn't, was not because I lifted my sunglasses. It was because Wes didn't know that it wasn't possible. Chloe may have had a few passing thoughts about us looking alike, but in all her years, she learned that surviving death was not reality. Wes, on the other hand, well heck, he probably still believed in Santa Claus.

I pictured Easton shaking his head in my mind. Disappointed. I was beginning to believe him all those times he told me I couldn't show myself to past loved ones. They don't understand, he'd say. I always believed I could make them, but shortly after I spoke to my dad in the hospital, his heart stopped beating. And now, when I smiled and winked at my little nephew, he immediately went into a tail spin. I frowned, closing the book in my lap and watched her car pull away. Easton was right about this rule. No more, I told myself.

That evening I ordered a couple of pizzas to the house after Tanner had dropped by, and looked like he wasn't leaving anytime soon. Instead, he sprawled out on our sofa, beer in hand.

"Make yourself comfortable," I said.

"I got a place!" Tanner announced. "Rented a home just the next neighborhood over. Only took me six minutes to get here, but that was probably because there was some construction on the main road. I bet when it clears, it will only take three. Or two!" Tanner raised his beer can to me.

"You're staying?" I asked. He had mentioned the possibility before the wedding, but really hadn't said much afterward. At least not to me. But I should have known, since he hadn't quite left our house yet, either.

"Oh yeah! Three amigos. Just like when we were kids,"

Tanner said, kicking off his shoes and putting his feet up on our coffee table. My eyes dropped to his dirty socks.

"Isn't that great news?" Easton asked.

"Yeah! Congratulations," I nodded.

"And I got all the sign-up info for the academy today, too," Tanner said.

Easton's eyes flickered between his brother and me, and then mine did the same.

"Oh, um, Beck, do you remember when we talked about me becoming a police officer?" Easton said.

I stared unblinkingly at him. Was he serious? Now? When we were going to have a baby? "You mean when we agreed you were too wimpy to become a police officer?" I asked, head cocked.

Tanner laughed, slapping his knee. "Good one, Bec!"

"Well, Tanner and I thought we could join the academy together . . ." Easton said, ignoring my original comment.

I glared at him, willing him to read my mind. Could Tethered Souls read each other's minds? I'd have to try. *Don't put your life on the line when you are going to be a father!*

"Come on, Bec, you can't expect Easton to just sit on the sofa? He's the man of the house now! He has to provide for his family! Am I right?" Tanner said.

Easton pointed to his brother and nodded in agreement. "Can't you provide for your *family* . . . by becoming an accountant? Or a real estate agent? Or literally anything . . . that doesn't put you in front of a bullet?" I asked. The brothers stared at me and then at each other. I could tell that Easton was feeding off Tanner's energy, and I didn't like it.

"Come on, Beck, I'm going to get that six-pack that you always wanted," Easton said.

"Yeah, come on, Bec," Tanner said.

I rolled my eyes. These misfits were impossible. "I mean, I can't tell you what to do, but—"

"Yeah!" Tanner raised his fist in the air and nearly spilled his beer. I rolled my eyes and glared at Easton.

"Everything will be OK," Easton said in a low voice. Our eyes locked for a moment, and by the time our contact had broken, I felt he was sincere. Not that he had any control over what would happen to him in the line of duty, but that possibly he had a plan. Or maybe Brooklyn had shared a dream with him. Either way, his blue eyes from across the living room were soothing, and at some point, I had to realize I couldn't control what happened in my life. Not with Easton, and not with our baby boy.

"All six abs?" I asked.

CHAPTER 15

My nausea grew worse, and vomiting in the morning became routine. It was miserable, and most days, I laid in bed until noon, thankful I had taken a semester off school for the wedding. But when the phone rang with my pregnancy test results, it made it all worthwhile. It was confirmed; I was, in fact, pregnant. The impossible made possible. It seemed to be a theme in my life. The second I got off the call with the nurse, I called Easton. I wanted to surprise him in some fancy way, but the moment was far too precious to hold on to until he got home. The phone rang three times before he picked up.

"Hello?" Easton answered the phone.

"I'm pregnant!" I blurted out.

"You are?"

"Yes!"

"Holy shit! Beck's pregnant!" Easton said, his voice away from the speaker.

"Wait! Don't tell anybody! It's bad luck until I hear the heartbeat!" I said.

". . . Or, nevermind," Easton said.

"Wait, so she is, or she isn't?" Tanner's muffled voice came through the phone.

"No, she really is!" Easton whispered.

I rolled my eyes. "I love you!" I said. It's all that mattered, anyway.

"I love you, too. I'll be home after we finish registering for the academy," Easton said.

"OK. Bye." I hung up the phone, a large grin wrapped around my face. I didn't know I felt this way. Not until my reaction to the nurse's call had I really detected my feelings as excitement. And in fact, it surprised me a little. I was going to be a mother. And I could hardly wait. A mini Easton, following me around all day. My imagination ran wild of a little boy—much like Wes with his shaggy hair—running through the backyard. It was so real. I swore I could see him straight through the glass slider. I had no idea this was where my life had been heading, but now that it was upon me, I couldn't imagine my purpose without it.

I slowly sat down on the sofa, my eyes still fixed on the figment of my imagination playing in the backyard. *I couldn't imagine my purpose without it.* And there it was. The answer. I would live my last life. I watched as the little boy playing in the yard dissipated like a cloud moving past the sky, and I was left with nothing but a sinking feeling of doom. If I had this baby, my life would be fulfilled. And if my life were lived to its full potential, then it would be my last. Easton would be right. Our baby would be left unprotected for centuries to come. I would have to believe deep down in my heart that there were people in this world that would do my job for me when I was gone.

Brooklyn dreamed of the day it would happen. The day we died. She said Easton wasn't the least concerned when she told him. And to be honest, neither was I. Not until now, until it was crucial that I lived forever. Brooklyn devised a plan to evade her premonition. There was only one way to accomplish it, though, and it was as simple as doing nothing at all. Keeping the status quo. What had worked for me in the past was surely going to work for me again. If I could just stay the same—let my fears hold me back from the things I really wanted to achieve and the people I wanted to love—then my life would never be enriched enough to be considered fulfilled. The box simply left unchecked. Simple. I'd been mediocre for as long as I remembered.

Brooklyn was worried when I told her I was getting married until she finally concluded that it wouldn't change much in Easton's and my life. We already lived together anyway and had been doing it for a year. We had loved each other in our past life too, and I still wound back here to live another life. But having a baby was a big change. It was a fork in the road, and we were pivoting. An alternative path altogether, and it sure wasn't the one I had been traveling down for the past two lives. Something told me that being mediocre would no longer work for me and that I'd need to come out of my comfort zone. If I were to shape a person's mind, core, and values ... I couldn't do it half-heartedly. This would be the greatest job I'd ever been given, and I couldn't afford not to give it my best.

Come to think of it, Easton would need to pivot also. While he hadn't lived his life in the shadow of fear quite as I had, he did have a hard time loving. Of course, that would come crashing down the moment he held our baby boy in his arms. Did that mean that his life would be fulfilled too? Was his three hundred years of wandering the same lonely path coming to an end? Was his tether going to fray? And possibly the most pressing matter, was that something that I needed to tell him?

I curled up on the sofa, laying on my side in the fetal position. Tears pricked my eyes, and eventually, they fell at will. I was ready to sacrifice my immortality if that was the cost for opening up my heart to this little baby, and I would do it fearlessly and wholeheartedly. But if I told Easton, would that meddle in his fate? Would he resent me, or the baby, for not living out eternity with him? Or would he simply live his last life too?

I hadn't been set on living forever, though it was something I was told I would do. The thought of traveling the world had become more enticing to me recently. But the possibility of it coming to an end was saddening. And it would be devastating if I weren't there to take care of my child in their next lives. My eyes grew tired from worry, and eventually, before Easton came home, I fell asleep on the sofa and succumbed to the nightmares of the unknown path I was on.

✱ ✱ ✱

Two very long weeks later, and I hadn't told Easton that I was dying all over again. But weren't we all? I looked around the waiting room at the OB-GYN's office. All of these people were dying; maybe not today—*probably* not today—but they were well on their way. The only difference between them and Easton and I was that he and I wouldn't quite complete the process. Honestly, it was like we failed to launch. We were stuck in some sort of endless time loop. But I knew the way out, and Brooklyn had made me promise not to speak of it. It wasn't my place to change someone's path, she would say, and I believed that.

Easton squeezed my hand when the nurse called us back. My stomach did flips, and my palms were a sweaty mess. Easton did what he could to calm me, but his jokes paled in comparison to the anxiety raging inside me. "Take a seat. I'm going to ask you some questions, and then Dr. Faye will be right with you," the nurse said.

I answered the nurse's questions as she took my blood pressure. We laughed when she stated I was nervous. I thought I had covered it up, but my blood pressure was through the roof. "You're going to put on this gown. Completely undress from the waist down. The opening will be in the back. Easton will have to wait out in the waiting room during the exam," the nurse said.

"Can't he stay?" I asked.

"I'm sorry, it's our policy that during the internal ultrasound, no guests in the room. It's a tight squeeze as it is. But he can come back for the following check-ups." The nurse walked Easton out, but not before he gave me a quick peck on the forehead. I smiled and waved him goodbye.

Then, I wrestled with the embarrassing smock. I sat on the exam chair and tried to tuck the paper-thin gown around my backside. I looked around the room while waiting for the doctor, swinging my feet with uncomfortable anticipation. *Should I have taken my socks off?*

A knock on the door sounded before it opened up slowly. "Hello, are you decent?" A man's voice asked from behind a curtain.

"Yes," I replied, checking my gown again.

The doctor pulled the curtain back, and I was immediately taken aback by his tall, broad, and ruggedly handsome stature. "Hello, I'm Dr. John Faye, and you must be . . . Becca Green?" he asked, peeking at his chart.

"That's me. . ." I said, cheeks flushing.

Dr. Faye greeted me, making my hand feel small and cold within his.

"So, is this your first pregnancy?" he asked.

"Yes," I said.

"How are you feeling? Any morning sickness?"

"Oh, yeah . . ." My skin heated. The doctor was twice my age, and his hair was in the first stages of turning grey, but if anything, it only made him more handsome.

"OK, well, that can be a good sign. It means your pregnancy hormones are strong. You've got a little fighter in there, I'm sure. And we're going to take a look today. Are you ready for that?" The doctor asked.

"Yes." I twisted my foot around the back of my leg as I clammed up.

"So this is an internal ultrasound wand; I will be using it to get a better look at the little bean since it's not large enough to see with the doppler just yet." My eyes grew wide at the sight of the large grey stick he held up. The doctor rolled backward on his chair and pushed a button near the door calling the nurse back into the room. "I'm going to have you lay down and scooch your bum to the end of the table," he said.

I took a moment to stare disbelievingly. I didn't know what to expect for today's appointment, but it definitely wasn't this. I laid on my back and closed my eyes tight, wishing my doctor wasn't as hot as he was. It made it so very wrong. "Just relax your knees," he said. The humiliation crowded out every other emotion rolling through my body. "Scooch down, a little more," he said. I scrunched my eyes tightly and moved down another inch. "Good. A little more. . ." I just about *died*.

Mortification ensued until something unexpected happened. "Oh, wow!" the doctor said. My eyes flung open, and I frantically sought out the nurse's face. Had she not been smiling, I might have had a heart attack.

"What? What is it?" I asked.

"Do twins run in your family?" The doctor asked.

"What?!"

"Well, if you look at the screen to your left . . ."

I whipped my head to the left and glared at the screen, but I could only see variations of grey matter. The screen could have been broken for all I could tell. "Do you see the two sacs?" Dr. Faye asked.

"No. I'm sorry, I don't. Did you say twins?" I asked, looking back at him.

"Here, why don't you sit up," he said, finishing the

exam and helping me upright. "Sometimes, two eggs can be fertilized—"

"But, you said twins?" I repeated.

The doctor sighed. "Yes. You are having twins. Congratulations." He smiled while the nurse wrote frantically on her chart. I took a deep breath, feeling somewhat lightheaded by the time I breathed out all the hot air.

"I'm sorry, I just… I don't understand," I said. But that's not what I meant. I understood how two eggs could be fertilized. I understood how one egg could divide into two. Twins were no mystery to me; but I never once considered it a possibility for me and my body. I only recently concluded that I wanted a baby at all. But two? I didn't know if I could take care of two kids.

"Do twins run in your family?" Dr. Faye asked again.

"No!" I scrunched my brows and shook my head. Then I remembered I was adopted. My genetics didn't come from my parents now, and not even from this lifetime. I thought back to my first family, and there were no twins that I recalled in their lines either. "No. . ." I repeated, my eyes off in the distance.

I finished talking with the doctor—no longer concerned with his rugged good looks—and finished dressing. I rolled the smock up in a ball and set it on the chair. When I walked out into the waiting room as white as a ghost, Easton popped to his feet. "Are you OK? Is everything OK?" he asked, searching my eyes.

"It's, um. It's . . . two. Twins . . . there's two of them . . ." I mumbled something incoherently.

"Twins?!" Easton's voice echoed in the small waiting room. The few patients there peeked up at us. "We're having twins!" Easton announced. A small applause erupted, and congratulations were expressed. I was barely aware of my surroundings as we walked out to the car. If there was any concern that my life would be fulfilled with the love of one child, there was undoubtedly no questioning that twice the love would bring my life to a complete stop. And this was something that I would need to tell Easton.

CHAPTER 16

The advice on the block was not to tell friends and family of your pregnancy until the second trimester. Got to make sure it "Sticks," they would say. Though, with how nauseous I was, I was pretty sure the stickiness of this pregnancy was like molasses. That's why we were going to tell Brooklyn and Tanner tonight when they came for dinner. Sure, Tanner already knew, but not officially. I was looking forward to seeing his best surprised face. I'd bet that it was terrible.

It was a perfect summer day, hot by morning and just bearable by the evening. It made me yearn for the days of dipping my feet in the pool as a kid. Easton would swim, of course, but I only got as deep as the second step. I smiled as I set the table with fancy napkin rings and peered outside to Easton by the barbecue. It was the first real dinner I'd host as a wife, and I wanted to make it special. Well, that and Brooklyn had been begging me to set her up with Tanner since the wedding. They had been lucky enough to run into each other here or there, but each time it was nothing but awkward. I had the feeling she liked Tanner a lot more than anyone in her recent years and perhaps recent lives. Tanner, on the other hand, played it cool, though he seemed interested enough.

The doorbell rang. I took one last glance at the dining table before answering the door. When I opened it, Brooklyn greeted me with large eyes that glistened with anticipation. She had a crush, alright. I could see her gaze flicker behind me, searching for Tanner. "Come in; he's out back," I said.

Brooklyn stepped in as she tugged on her sundress. It hugged all the right places and was a perfect choice for a summer barbeque. "How do I look? Do I look OK?" she asked.

"Stop, you look amazing. Any guy would be lucky to have you," I said. It was the truth. Brooklyn was a babe, and not only that, she was smart and caring.

"Right, no, I know. I'm not nervous or anything. Just asking," Brooklyn said with shifty eyes and tense shoulders. I smiled.

"Right," I agreed. "Can I get you a drink? I have a seltzer, cold and bubbly."

"Yes, that would be great. So, what have you been up to? I haven't seen you much lately. Is married life all that consuming?" Brooklyn asked though I could tell that her thoughts were elsewhere.

I slid her a seltzer and tied my long hair back in a bun. "I know, I'm sorry. I've been . . . gardening," I said, thinking back to the time I considered buying lilies at the market, but passed on them.

"Oh, I didn't know you had a green thumb. You will have to show me," Brooklyn said, opening her drink. I chewed on the inside of my cheek as her eyes searched the kitchen counter. "You're not having one?"

I swallowed. This conversation was too much work, and I wanted to tell her about the pregnancy at the dinner table; not here, not now. "I'm going to have one a little later," I said.

"Have one now," she pressed.

"Do you want to go outside? See Tanner?" I asked.

"Yeah!" Brooklyn shimmied her shoulders and headed for the back slider. She turned just before I rounded the kitchen counter. "Bring your drink," she said as she disappeared outside. I sighed, then turned around and snatched a seltzer from the refrigerator.

The air was thick with heat and the sky still bright as I joined Easton, Tanner, and Brooklyn near the barbeque. The tension was high, and the conversation had stalled. I cracked open the top to my seltzer, and both boys stared at me with knitted brows. I smiled at them with narrowed eyes until someone dared to break the silence. "So, I hear you two are joining the police academy?" Brooklyn said before taking a sip of her drink. I mimicked her, raising my seltzer to my lips and then pulling it away. I assumed nobody was watching me that closely, and from their peripheral vision, I was most likely pulling this thing off. If anything were to blow my cover, it was going to be Easton's shifty eyes.

"Yeah, you're looking at two of Clover's newest officers right here!" Tanner slapped Easton's back.

"Wait, you already did it?" Brooklyn asked.

"Oh no. But we signed up, so there's that," Tanner said.

"Oh, wow. That's going to be great. I can't wait to see you in a uniform—I mean you guys. I mean . . . not you Easton . . ." Brooklyn sipped her drink and looked around the yard, her cheeks red. Had I really been drinking my seltzer, I would have spit it out right then and there. I'd never seen Brooklyn so awkward and from the look on her face, she hadn't been used to it either. I glanced at Easton and raised my drink back to my lips and winked at him. "What are you doing?" Brooklyn asked.

I whipped my head over to her. "What?" I asked.

"Are you seriously pretending to drink that seltzer?" she asked.

"Oh, that. . ." I bit my bottom lip, stalling. It wasn't how I wanted to tell her. But after I glanced around our back yard and saw no tell-tale signs of my gardening, I decided it was time to drop the act. "So, I have something to tell you . . ."

"Stop—" Brooklyn started.

"I'm pregnant!" I said in a high-pitched voice, not out of excitement but out of the uncertainty of how it would be received. Brooklyn stared, her face expressionless. I'm not sure why, but I felt like I was in trouble. She took an extra-long drink, finishing her can. I quickly glanced at Easton, and I could tell that he was uncomfortable too.

"Well, I already knew, but officially . . . congratulations," Tanner said before reaching out for a hug.

"He already knew?" Brooklyn said, finally breaking her silence and confirming that, in fact, I was in some sort of trouble with my best friend.

"Well, no. He had his theories and all, but—" I said, pulling out of Tanner's arms.

"No, I knew. Easton told me," Tanner said, making the whole thing worse. I slapped my thigh and gave him a sideways glare. Was it not obvious what was happening here? I caught the slightest glance of Easton's smirk before he turned back to the barbeque. "So, what are you going to name them?" he asked. Tanner asked.

My stomach sank, and I closed my eyes, briefly pinching the bridge of my nose. This couldn't have gone any worse. "Them?" Brooklyn asked, looking between Tanner and me.

"I. I. I'm having twins," I stammered.

Brooklyn smiled a wide toothy grin that didn't come close to touching her eyes. "Congratulations, you guys. I'm so happy for you to have chosen that path," she said. I startled when she grabbed the seltzer out of my hand and started on it. I watched her as she guzzled my untouched drink. "What about you, Tanner? Do you want kids?" she asked. My eyes flickered to his.

"Oh, well yeah—" Brooklyn shook her head no, "—Maybe, no. No." Tanner was quick to change his answer, shaking his head no alongside Brooklyn's.

"Hey, I'm just going to check on the . . . salad. Easton?" I asked, calling his attention away from the barbeque. He followed me into the kitchen, shutting the slider behind him. "What was that?" I asked the second the door closed.

"I know. Why was she mad? Think she's jealous?"

"Jealous? No, why would she be jealous? I mean Tanner. He's practically throwing me under the bus. I thought he knew it was a secret?"

"Well, yeah. But the secret's out," Easton said, confused. I let out a loud audible sigh. Why didn't guys understand that it was never straightforward with us girls? He was supposed to act like he was surprised so that Brooklyn didn't get her feelings hurt for not knowing first. "Am I missing something?" Easton asked.

"No," I said. *Yes.* He was missing something—a very large something—that I couldn't explain right now. I peeked through the slider to see Brooklyn reaching out and touching Tanner's shoulder. "New plan," I said, eyes on the flirting.

"There was an old plan?" Easton asked.

"Stay with me here, Easton! We need them to fall in love." If Brooklyn fell for Tanner, she'd forget all about how I derailed her plan to be best friends *forever.*

"We do?" Easton asked.

"Yeah." Clearly, we weren't on the same page.

"Why?"

"I don't know. . ." *So, she wasn't mad at me?* "Because she likes him?" I said.

Easton shrugged. "Fair enough. What's the plan then?" he asked, steepling his chin and watching the couple by the barbeque.

"Well, we can start by giving them some alone time?" I said. Easton nodded and pulled up a seat at the kitchen counter. "You're just going to sit there like that?"

"Yeah, was I supposed to be doing something else?"

"Well, you can't make it obvious! Here, toss the salad," I said, pulling out the salad that needed our desperate attention.

"So, what do you really think is going on with her? Why wouldn't she be excited?" Easton mixed the salad as I threw in berries and walnuts.

"She's worried things will change between us, and we will drift apart," I said, feeling sad for the inevitable change. I was deflated by how she reacted, but my heart hurt knowing why she did it even more.

"Well, that's ridiculous. I mean, unless she has a thing against babies, there's no reason you two can't still be best friends," Easton said. I wished it were as simple as that. Maybe Brooklyn should give up the act and finish what she started, too. Maybe we all should live our last life . . .

"Shit, here they come. Act natural!" I said, doing anything but. Easton frowned and picked up the salad tongs again.

"Oh, hey . . . We were just tossing the salad," I hated myself the second the words left my mouth.

"OK," Brooklyn said on her way to the refrigerator. She pulled out another seltzer, and I immediately knew it was going to be one of those nights. Although, this was the first time I wouldn't be able to drink away the sorrows alongside her.

When dinner was ready, Brooklyn and Tanner had drunk enough to put them on a different level altogether. They were loud, clumsy, and the flirting was terrible. It wasn't the romantic start I wanted for them, but it was outside of my control. Easton and I observed as the night went sideways on us, but only he found it amusing.

"Did Easton tell you we had a physical assessment today?" Tanner said from across the table.

"How'd that go?" Brooklyn asked.

"He's got some work to do," Tanner laughed, and Brooklyn wailed.

"It's training . . . and you need it too," Easton said.

"Is this where it ends, Easton?" Brooklyn said, and the way she stared at Easton made me believe she wasn't talking about his path to becoming a police officer.

"No, Brooklyn. This is only the beginning," Easton replied, picking up on her shift.

"That's what you think. But your wrong," Brooklyn said.

"It's just training. Haven't you ever worked out before?" Easton asked.

"You can't train your way out of this mess." The room fell silent as Easton and Brooklyn glared at each other. The way they fought, they could have been brother and sister. And now that I thought about it, maybe they had been in another life.

"It's OK, little brother. We will beef up those spaghetti arms. Ain't no chicken legs holding my bro back!" Tanner said.

"OK, first of all, Tanner, I'm older than you—" The moment Easton said it, I could tell he realized he was fighting an uphill battle.

"By sixteen days—" he pointed at Easton with his breadstick.

"And second of all, these aren't chicken legs! I don't know why you keep calling them that. I'm a man of steel. Just ask Beck!"

"Do you mean Becca?" Brooklyn asked. *Oh no. What was she doing?* Easton sighed, clearly not happy with Brooklyn's attempts to derail the night. "Surely you don't mean *Everly?*"

My stomach dropped. Easton slammed his hands down on the table and popped to his feet.

"Who's Everly?" Tanner asked, looking around the table. I bit my lip, my heart pounding.

"Brooklyn! Can I talk to you outside?" I asked sharply. She rolled her eyes but followed me into the backyard. The air was still hot, and it helped to take the edge off the icy conversation inside. "What are you trying to do?" I snapped, harsher than intended.

Brooklyn popped a hand on her hip and laid into me. "You are a liar!" I flinched back. Her tone piercing. "You and I were a team. You told me that you would never leave me. And when you married Easton, you promised me nothing would change between us. But here we are, Becca. You went and changed the plan. And you didn't even talk to me about it. And then you told Tanner before you told me? Do I mean nothing to you?"

"No, that's not—"

"You and I were a team! Did you ever think how you would impact my future if you broke our pact? Did you even think about me at all?" her voice rising with fury.

"Brooklyn, I'm sorry, but—"

"But, what? You made your choice. You dug your grave. I can't help you anymore, Becca."

"I don't need your help!"

"Well, don't think I'm going to stick around to see how it ends for you." Brooklyn's eyes turned sober, making it hurt twice as much.

"That's . . . like sixty years from now, you can't be my friend for the next sixty years?" I asked.

A tear fell off Brooklyn's cheek, and I wasn't sure if it was because she was angry or sad. Maybe a little of both. Easton popped his head out of the slider, and I wondered how much they heard inside. "Dinner is cold," he said.

"This won't end well for you, Becca," she said as she wiped her cheek and breezed past me. Dinner continued just as terrible as the first half, but Brooklyn had turned her attention to Tanner making embarrassing and sometimes crude comments this time. By the end of the long night, Brooklyn had fallen asleep on our sofa, and Easton drove Tanner home. I sat at the dinner table with my hand on my tummy, staring at the untouched food, wondering where the night had gone wrong. It was my first time hosting dinner, and I wanted the night to go perfectly. It was to be a celebration of life but turned into quite literally the opposite. Brooklyn was mad at me for choosing love over immortality. I picked up a cold dinner roll and rolled it around in my hand. Had I really chosen this for myself? Or was the path chosen for me long ago?

I had just started to clean the kitchen when Easton came home. He stood in the entryway staring at Brooklyn for a moment. "Do you want me to take her home?" he asked.

"No. She lives too far. She can just stay here tonight. I'm sure she'll leave in the morning."

"Right." Easton picked up the plates from the dinner table and brought them to the sink. "Barefoot and pregnant," he said.

I smirked at him. "Sorry tonight was such a disaster," I said.

"It's OK. I know I don't have chicken legs." I laughed a little too loud, and Brooklyn stirred on the sofa. "So, she knows about Everly?" he asked, a little surprised.

"Yeah, well, I told her. I had to. I should have said something to you earlier. Sorry."

Easton shrugged it off. "She believed you?" he asked.

"It was the only thing that made sense with her dreams and all. I told her that our death was in the past, and she had nothing to worry about. It actually helped strengthen our relationship." Easton didn't know that I spoke to Brooklyn about being tethered, let alone that she was tethered herself. I wasn't sure why it was so important for her to keep secret, but I would not say anything if it was important to her.

"That's surprising. It's never turned out that way for me. It usually just blows up in my face. I lose my friend. Always." I felt terrible. Especially when I thought back to how my nephew reacted at the park. But I held that information back too. It seemed like I did that a lot lately.

"Well, I'm glad you have such a good friend that she would stand by you, even when you tell her something as impossible as this. But she sure was upset tonight."

"She just feels like I'm leaving her behind. I don't agree

with it, but I can understand where she's coming from. She's told me I was like a sister to her, and she hasn't had that since her very first—" I froze. My hands still under the running water.

"First, what?" Easton asked. I'd said too much. It wasn't my place to tell.

"First grade. Since she was in first grade." I started washing the dishes again. Easton and I continued talking till the kitchen was clean, and then I was ready to hit the bed like a ton of bricks. My eyes burned, and I was more tired doing daily tasks now that I was simultaneously building two people from scratch. I waited in the hall for Easton as he walked out into the living room and turned off the lights. Brooklyn stirred once more, and then I heard her . . .

"Goodnight, killer . . ."

CHAPTER 17

Goosebumps prickled my skin as I stood in the dark hallway. There was a bitter moment of stillness before Easton's footsteps padded down the hall. Whatever he felt, whatever he wanted to say back to Brooklyn, it took a lot of strength to hold inside. I felt the ice as Easton passed by me. Closing the door softly behind me, I watched Easton's silhouette disappear into the restroom. The lights from the bathroom lit up a portion of our bedroom, but I stood still in the shadows. Torn between being a good friend and being a good wife.

We got ready for bed in silence, and after lying by his side, unable to close my eyes, I rolled onto my side to see Easton still awake. "Brooklyn means well. I know she came off a little harsh tonight, but she means well," I whispered.

"What are you not telling me?" he asked bluntly.

I sighed, knowing the time had come. "I wasn't supposed to say anything—"

"But I'm your husband. That rule doesn't apply when we're married." He may have been right. I didn't know. Maybe it was a grey area, but I felt that hiding the truth about my friend's life was doing more harm than good. So, I told him.

"Brooklyn is a Tethered Soul, like us," I whispered. It was only the beginning. A long moment passed as Easton's mind bent and folded in on itself. I found it odd he didn't blink. Not once.

"That's impossible," he whispered back.

"No. It's not. I mean, it was impossible for me to be tethered, but here I am."

"Right. But Brooklyn's not tethered, Beck."

"Yes. She is . . ."

"I would know. I would sense it. She's not. She's lying to you. And the real question is, why?" Taken aback by his comment, I was conflicted about defending her while I felt the need to explore the plausible reasons why my friend would deceive me in such a way. There was none. She'd been a great friend to me.

"Well, maybe you don't know as much as you claim," I said.

"I know enough to know she's lying to you. I'll tell you that much. I'm going to talk to her tomorrow, this is ridiculous—"

"No!"

"I should just talk to her now." Easton sat up, and I reached out, grabbing his shoulder.

"No. Please don't," I begged.

Easton ran his hands through his hair, and even through

the darkness, I could see the distress he was in. I could feel it in the air. He was trying to protect me. Trying to do right by me. I hated myself for putting him in this position. The tension stretched between us and slinked down my body. I was tired beyond belief, but I acted out of instinct, leaning over and kissing his neck. My intention wasn't to keep him in bed there with me, though it did that too.

In the morning, I woke up stiff and groggy. Easton made coffee, and the clanking of coffee mugs woke Brooklyn on the sofa. She moaned and brought her hands to her head. I poured myself a decaf coffee and smiled at her misery. Somehow it felt better to know that I wasn't the only one suffering from nausea and a headache.

Easton and I sat down in the living room, and I thought it was kind of him to bring her a cup of coffee, even though she accused him of being a killer just the night before. It was something I wouldn't have been able to do so easily. She smiled at him apologetically and then took the mug. Her head hung as she rubbed the sleep from her eyes. And eventually, she began her apology. "Sorry about last night, guys," she said . . . *That's it?* I waited for more to come, but she felt her debt was free.

"So, you know that Becca Reed is Everly Beck, huh?" Easton asked. Brooklyn's brows rose, and she nodded slowly, preparing herself for the long talk ahead of her.

"And now, Becca Green," I mumbled to myself.

"If you knew Becca was Beck, and Beck was Becca, then you would know how important it is to keep that a secret. Why would you bring it up in front of Tanner?" Easton asked.

"Tanner wasn't going to find out. Plus, who really cares if your older brother finds out about Beck?" Brooklyn frowned.

"He's not my older brother—"

"He's *actually* . . . Easton's younger—" I started.

"Whatever. He doesn't know," Brooklyn said, cutting us both off.

Easton shook his head, frustrated with her energy. And I'd have to say he wasn't the only one. "Look, Brooklyn, I know you're upset with me for getting pregnant, but I didn't choose this. I didn't even think it was possible. I swear," I said.

"See, that's the problem, you guys. You're the blind leading the blind. How are you supposed to survive this if you're only listening to him? He doesn't know what he's talking about half the time. You guys don't understand that I'm trying to help you. But you make it so damn hard! Hell, if it weren't for me, you two wouldn't have even found each other again," Brooklyn said.

"What are you talking about?" Easton asked, brows furrowing.

"I knew you were looking for her. I saw it in my dreams. And I saw Becca was lost without you. But do you know how hard it is to make someone fall in love with somebody they can't remember?" Brooklyn rubbed her temple.

"Actually, yeah, I do," Easton said.

"Why? Why did you help us get back to one another?"

"Because she was lost. And she was my friend—" Brooklyn spoke to Easton but stared directly at me with her deep brown eyes. "She's the only friend I've had for so, so long."

"How long?"

Brooklyn pried her eyes off me and looked to Easton, her eyes softening. She sniffed in a broken breath of air and then began a story even I had never heard. "I was born in 1450 in Early Modern Europe. I was a gifted child. Dreaming big dreams that told the future. By the time I was five, it was clear that my future was anything but bright. They called me witch." Brooklyn took a sip of her coffee, and her eyes fell unfocused to her lap.

"Even my own family was afraid of me." Brooklyn cleared her throat, pushing past the memories. "In 1457, at only seven years old, I was burned at the stake in front of my entire village. I watched as my very own sister cheered along with the angry villagers as my skin lit fire and I burned from the outside in. To this day, it was the most horrific, excruciating death."

Goosebumps covered my arms, and shivers split down my back. My chest heavy with sorrow for what she had experienced. I knew she was tethered, but that was about all she had told me. Now I saw why she didn't want others to know. It was a story she rarely wanted to relive.

"Born again the same day, I woke in a wicker basket on a doorstep. As I grew, my dreams were more vivid, and I often spoke of them when I was young. My parents were more loving than my first and shielded me from the villagers until I made one fatal mistake. I ran into my sister. All my rage poured out of me as the memories flooded my mind. She'd betrayed me more than anyone had before. I ran to her, telling her about the terrible man she would marry and all the horrible things he would do to her. I told her how she would die, and I screamed the day it would happen. She took one look at me amongst the villagers and called out at the top of her lungs. 'Witch!' she screamed. I was taken immediately. That's when the cycle started."

"Oh my god, Brooklyn. I'm so, so sorry," I said, my hand heavy over my heart.

"It was over two hundred years later when the infamous Salem Witch Trials began, and by then, they were hanging witches, not burning them. I used my dreams to warn the folk of their impending doom. Time after time, they would rat me out, and we would hang together. That's when I decided I wouldn't use my gift to help others anymore. I became cold-hearted. I had to. It was the only way I could survive. But it was no way to live." Brooklyn said, and Easton nodded with a heavy heart.

Brooklyn took a deep, shaky breath and shrugged. "I'm not that way anymore, though. I only wasted a few lives before I started helping people again. And to be honest, having a friend like Becca has helped me a lot. I wanted to help her find her soulmate. Her love. And when I met you, Easton, I wanted to help you too." Brooklyn's voice was shaky.

"I don't understand. Why do you think that's all going to change? What does having a baby have to do with any of this?" Easton asked. My stomach dipped, and I knew right then and there that I didn't want Easton knowing that fate was calling. Brooklyn's eyes flickered to me, and I gave a quick shake of the head. I didn't have it in my heart to tell him my second chance was fleeting.

"Our friendship isn't doomed, I just felt . . . threatened. Like I would lose her. I mean, having a baby just takes up of all your time. Who is going to go shopping with me and such?" Brooklyn joked. "I'm going to get some more coffee. Do you want any?" She asked.

I mouthed "Thank you" to her, and she responded with a small smile.

"Yes, please." Easton handed her his mug and then turned his focus on me. "But, Brooklyn, one more thing. Why did you call me a killer?" Easton continued to pry.

"Well, you know. I told you that part. That you two died in my dream. Remember? I told you."

"Yeah. But that was our past life. I thought you knew that?" Easton said.

"Yeah. Um, Becca told me that bit. And you know, my dreams change all the time," Brooklyn said from the kitchen.

"So, everything is good? As far as your dreams go?" Easton asked.

"Oh, yeah. I haven't even had one since I talked to you last! That was before you asked Becca to marry you, remember? It's honestly nothing." Brooklyn came back into the room with two mugs of coffee. She wasn't being honest. I knew that much. She had dreams every night. Sometimes about people she hadn't even met yet. And they always came true. Every single time.

"Thanks," he said, taking the coffee. "Brooklyn?"

Easton's expression shifted. "If you 're a Tethered Soul, then how come I can't see it?"

"See it?" Brooklyn cocked her head to the side.

Easton nodded. "I can see just how long one's lived. I can see the pain they carry like rings inside a tree trunk. It burns around them like a burning ball of embers."

"Oh, that. That's not what you think it is, Easton," Brooklyn smirked.

"What are you talking about?"

"Hazy? Kind of yellow, orange glow? Sometimes angry looking?"

Easton shrugged. "Yeah. It's how we Tethered Souls know each other. And you don't have it." Easton's tone became accusatory, and I slinked back into my chair.

"Let me ask you this, do you see that on Becca?" They both turned to me, and my eyes dropped to the floor.

"Well, no—but that's only because she's young. There aren't years of pain there, let alone much memory of it," Easton said, and I recoiled. Though it was true, I didn't like being talked about in terms of what I had and hadn't remembered.

"Exactly. She's not *tortured*, Easton. And neither am I. What that warm haze really means is that you are a Tortured Soul. A Tortured Soul can be a Tethered Soul, and more often than not, they are. It takes centuries to build up that kind of pain. The kind that is so deep it invades your energy. But what you fail to see is, a Tethered Soul doesn't have to be a tortured one."

"What—What are you talking about?" Easton's forehead creased with disbelief, and I didn't know what I had thought about it all. I knew one thing, though. I wasn't tortured. The thought of living forever wasn't negative to me at all, and I struggled to see how it ever could be.

"While it's true that I was tortured for many, many lives, I'm not anymore. I've made peace with my past. I no longer want to move on from it. Honestly, it's what makes me who I am, and I think I'm pretty great. I want to live forever! I'm happy, and you can't see that smoldering ember around me, Easton, because it doesn't exist in me." My eyes flickered to Easton.

"And you? You're happy too?" Easton asked me, his eyes holding my own.

"I . . . I mean, you always talk about how it's a curse, and I'm just not sure I feel that way."

"You don't?" Easton was taken aback. "God, Beck. You used to be so tortured. You used to be afraid of the dark because that's when you would be alone with your thoughts. You used to hurt yourself because the physical pain was easier to take than the pain in your heart. Don't you remember any of that? You don't carry that with you?" Easton asked.

"Honestly, I don't remember ever feeling that way. I think it's sad that I ever did. I think it's sad that people feel like that now. But if you asked me if I thought getting to live forever was a curse, I just don't think it is, and I might go as far as to say it could be a gift. I mean, I'm having babies. It has to be a gift, right?" I asked.

Easton nodded his head slowly, then looked back to Brooklyn. "So, all the Tethered Souls I've seen before," Easton began.

"Those are just the ones who don't understand yet. They're lost," Brooklyn said, setting down her empty cup of coffee.

"Lost Souls. . ." Easton said beneath his breath.

"Yeah. Like you. . ."

"Like me?" he asked.

"Yeah. You feel like there's no point; you want to move on but can't. You don't know your purpose here." Brooklyn shrugged like it was simple, and Easton nodded his head, deep in his own thought.

"I do feel that way," he said.

"Yeah." Brooklyn ran her hands through her hair, and I could tell she was getting ready to leave.

"I'm a Lost Soul . . ." Easton said to himself, eyes unfocused in the middle of the room. It was going to be a long day. It was then, when I knew we made the right decision not to tell him about the way out. I wasn't sure he could handle it. Would he race to make his life perfect so he could leave this world behind? Would it be disingenuous? Or would he sabotage himself like I had planned to all along so he could stay behind and care for our children? I had made my decision, but I believed it was best for him to make his on his own and in due time.

"Well, I think that's my cue. I'm going to go. Oh, one more thing. Can I still call you Becca? Or—" Brooklyn weighed both her hands in the air.

"Yeah, oh yeah! Um . . .?" I furrowed my brows, trying to think back to when Brooklyn had become a popular name.

"Don't you dare call me, Beatrix!" Brooklyn said,

pointing her finger at me. And had Easton not looked so sad, I might have laughed out loud.

"Promise," I said, opening the front door, my eyes still large with shock. *Beatrix.*

"Love ya," Brooklyn said, passing by and kissing me on the cheek. "Oh, and do me a favor, dear, give Tanner my number!"

CHAPTER 18

All the leaves had turned orange and fell to the ground. Now the trees were nothing more than naked branches in the frigid winter air. Easton had packed on quite a bit of muscle training to become a police officer, and my belly had grown to an astronomical size. I was riddled with back aches, heartburn, and a terrible case of the waddles. But at least the nausea had broken and never returned.

My appointments with Dr. Faye had all been great, and when the time came for him to disclose the twin's sexes, I chickened out at the last minute. I covered my eyes as he laughed. He ended up writing it down on a piece of notepaper and stuffed it in an envelope for me to take home in case it kept me up at night. He said it happened often, and he didn't want a call in the wee hours of the morning unless I was in labor. And you know what? It did keep me up that night. And had I not thrown that envelope in the trash when I walked out of his office, I would have ripped it open the very first night.

Brooklyn and Tanner had started officially dating after a re-do dinner at our house that ended with a goodnight kiss. It worked out kind of perfectly, because they ended up spending a lot of time at our house, and it felt like we were a family. In time, Brooklyn and I asked Easton if we could tell Tanner about our past lives, but he had a firm opinion on that, and since they were brothers, we had to let it go. She ended up telling him about some of her dreams, though, and he thought they were quite interesting. Brooklyn claimed he just didn't understand, and maybe it was better that we never told him about being tethered.

I thought about baby names often and had quite a list going. Brooklyn liked to sneak god-awful names on the list when I wasn't looking. And one time, I wrote Beatrix on there as a joke. She didn't find it as funny as I did. I spent a lot of time at the park, reading. Chloe and Wes hadn't come very often since he called me Everly, and I didn't blame them. But today, when I sat there with Brooklyn, I had a feeling in the pit of my gut that they might show. Brooklyn told me it was just indigestion.

"Do you remember when you told Easton that your dreams changed all the time?" I said, before taking a sip of my hot cocoa.

"Yeah."

"Was there any truth in that?"

"No. They never change. And often, as the event approaches, the dream becomes more frequent."

"Have you had the dream of me dying again? You know, since the first time?"

"No. It was just the one time," Brooklyn said.

"Would you tell me if you did?" I asked. I knew the second she paused that I would never get the full truth from her. I wondered how much she hid from me, even to this day.

"Honey, I'm going to tell you what I think you need to hear. And most likely, not an ounce more," Brooklyn said. At least she was honest.

"Why did you think we could change my fate and live forever if you had already had the dream?" I asked.

Brooklyn shrugged. "I guess I thought it was worth a shot. I mean, I know the formula. The ticket out of here . . . I just figured that if you knew it too, you would make a different choice for yourself. But you are so stubborn, Becca. You were always going to do your own thing." Brooklyn rolled her eyes like I was the most exhausting friend on this planet, and I smiled behind my cocoa.

"You mean like, I would just live the most boring life ever known to man? Or like, I wouldn't bring my pregnancy to term?" I asked, the thought leaving a sour taste in my mouth.

"Yeah. It's a choice, you know. I just didn't expect you to choose them over yourself or Easton."

I frowned. It was honest but cutting. They definitely heard it, too, because I got a sharp kick to the ribs. I moaned and twisted in on the bench. "Well, I do. I choose them. And I'd do it all over again."

Brooklyn chuckled. "You haven't even met them. . ."

"I don't have to!" I rubbed my belly.

"You don't? What if they're assholes?" Brooklyn laughed.

I rolled my eyes. She clearly didn't have the motherly instincts that I had. But before I snapped something rude back to her, I remembered a time before I was pregnant. I probably would have thought the same thing. "They probably will be," I said, causing both Brooklyn and I to laugh. "Oh, stop, stop! I can't laugh anymore. It hurts too much. It all hurts!" I choked out as I looked for a place to set my hot cocoa.

"Ohh, Becca. What am I going to do with you?" Brooklyn asked, wrapping an arm around me. I smiled at her and opened my mouth when a flicker of movement caught my eye.

"I knew it!" I said.

"Is that them?"

"Yeah, only that's Everly, my niece, and the little one is Wes. Chloe must be busy today," I said, watching them get out of the car.

"Awe, he's so cute! And she looks a lot like you. She's got your coloring, that's for sure," Brooklyn said.

"Yeah, I know."

"Well, hey, I've got to run. I told Tanner I would meet him at the police academy for lunch today." Brooklyn gathered her bag and stood up. "Thanks for the cocoa."

"Anytime. I'm going to stay here for a bit and read. Tell Easton I said hi."

"Ha, *read* . . . You know you don't read when you're here."

"I do! Sometimes," I said, smiling.

I waved Brooklyn goodbye and then turned my attention back to my niece. She looked like a young adult. Maybe graduating high school soon? And she did look like me. A lot more so when I was younger. I wondered if it was hard for my mom or brother to watch her grow up. Wes turned his head in my direction right as a sharp pain stabbed into my side. I pushed my hand into the cramp and breathed through it, all too aware that he had seen my face again. As the cramp subsided, I saw Wes tugging on my niece's sweatshirt.

By the look on his face, it was time to go. The last thing I wanted was another disturbance. The poor boy probably had nightmares. I stood up, and a gush of warm water soaked my jeans. I twisted around to see my hot cocoa still full on the bench next to me. I grabbed my tummy. It wasn't long before I gathered my water had broken, and I was going into labor. I still had another month until I was full term, but my doctor told me it wasn't uncommon to deliver early when you were carrying twins. I took nearly two steps towards my truck when a contraction hit, and I called out. Bringing attention to myself was not what I wanted to do. Not when the only people at the park were my niece and nephew. But that's exactly what happened. First, it was Everly. Then, Wes came running across the playground.

"Oh my god. Oh my god. What do I do? Oh, shit—" Everly panicked, placing her hand on my back. I felt a zing of electricity pass through her touch. It was my body recognizing her as my family, and I wondered if she felt it too.

"I'm good. I'm totally OK. I'm just going to drive myself to the hospital," I said, adjusting my oversized sunglasses and tugging at my scarf.

"Can you even drive?" Everly looked back to the fluid that covered the bench. Her expression covered in worry.

"Oh, yeah." My voice became more and more strained as I felt another stir of tightness approaching.

"OK. I'm just going to help you to your truck."

"That would be great," I said, waddling to the parking lot. It was clear to see which vehicle was mine. It was the only other vehicle in sight and right in front of hers. We headed straight for it. "Ahh," I called out, bending over in pain.

"Shit. Shit. Call 9-1-1! Wes, call 9-1-1!" Everly shouted.

"No! No. You. You don't. Need to. Do that," I huffed. "Ahh!" I bent over violently, propelling my sunglasses off my face. Wes hurried to pick them up. I knew the trouble I was in when he saw my face, and I only hoped that my niece hadn't been shown many photos of me. Perhaps she was too stressed out to notice. One could only hope.

"I think I need to drive you. Yeah. I'm going to drive you," she said.

"No, you don't need—"

"You can't drive! You can barely walk!" She had a good point there. I stood as straight as I could, taking baby steps to the parking lot. But when we approached her car and my truck, she was obviously right, and I couldn't drive in my condition. She opened her car door, and I slowly sat in her passenger seat. Wes climbed in the back, where he sat on a booster. "OK. Just hang on."

Everly took off, and I nearly bashed my head into the window. She was a terrible driver. I spread my hands out, one on the dash and one gripping the overhead handle, bracing myself. Between contractions, I thought about how I ended up in my niece's car—and more importantly—how my brother survived teaching this girl to drive. "My name's Everly, and that back there is my little brother Wes," she said.

"Hi," I choked out a breathless reply. I wanted to tell her I knew who she was. I wanted to talk to her for hours.

"What's your name?" she asked.

I had to stop and think about it, which was difficult when my body felt like it was trying to split in two. Beck would be too incriminating, and Everly was surely out the window. "Becca! Ahh!" I cried, gripping the overhead handle. Everly stepped on the gas, and we all but peeled out, rounding the corner into the hospital parking lot. I didn't know what was worse, the fear of inexperienced driving, or the two little people trying to break out of my body. "Thank you," I whispered. My voice disappearing under the pain.

"OK, little man, we've got to help Becca into the hospital. Can you help me?"

"Yeah! I'm gonna help!" Wes said.

I opened my door and swung my legs out of the car, my

niece and nephew helping to pull me to my feet. Gravity was not my friend, but Everly did what she could to help support me. Wes stuck by her side, gripping a fist full of her sweater. We were almost to the emergency entrance when the large glass doors opened, and a nurse with a wheelchair rushed to our aid. "Ahhh," I groaned, unable to sit until the contraction passed. Everly rubbed my back, and tears spilled from my eyes. Though they weren't the kind of tears that fell from the searing pain, they had been the kind that fell when you reunite with family you hadn't seen in far too long. The level of love and comfort I had with my niece and nephew—even never having spoken to them before—was far greater than anything I had experienced with a friend. There was something deep and raw between us that ran through my veins, and I wondered if Everly felt the connection, too. I knew the little man did.

"Good luck!" Everly called out as the nurse rolled me away.

"Luck!" Wes echoed.

I craned my neck to look at them one last time before the doors closed, but that involved a full body twist that I was incapable of. I muttered something inaudible that turned into a full sob. I had come so close. I only wished I could convey what they had meant to me; now . . . *then*. I'd say it too if I didn't think I would scare them with my words from beyond the grave.

"Is there somebody I can call dear?" the nurse asked. I'd lost my chance, was all I could think. "Dear, is there somebody I can call for you?"

Easton! I patted my pockets and the side of my

wheelchair. I didn't have my phone, my bag . . . nothing. "I don't, I don't know his number," I cried, searching and researching the same pockets. "It's on speed dial. I don't know it . . ." I said. How could I be so *stupid*?

"It's OK. We'll get you checked in, and I'm sure it's on file. We'll find it and call for you. What is the name of the person you are trying to contact?"

"Easton. Easton Green. He's my husband!"

"OK, dear. We'll call Easton then," the nurse reassured me.

Checking in was fast. I was placed in a room and monitored by several people, all who were incredibly nice. I was doing well keeping myself calm until a nurse came in to update me on Easton. "Hello, dear. My name is Judy, and I've been trying to reach your husband for you. He's not answering his phone. Is there someone else we can call?" she asked.

"He's at the police academy. Can you call them? There's only one, and it's in Decord City," I said.

"I'll give it a shot, and I'll let you know what they say," Judy said before disappearing from the room. I closed my eyes, hoping he'd be here shortly, but Decord City was an hour away, and I didn't want to wait that long to see him. I was going to have these babies all alone.

"Becca?" a small voice called from the hall. I opened my eyes to see Everly and Wes standing in the entryway. "You left your bag in my car," she said.

Immediately I began crying again. I waved them to come in, and I could tell that my emotional state made her somewhat uncomfortable, but I couldn't stop myself. Wes jumped on my bed, holding out the sunglasses I'd dropped at the park.

"Wes, no!" Everly snapped.

"It's OK," I said, sniffling. "Thank you, little man. That's so thoughtful of you," I said, careful not to wink at him again.

"You look like Everee," Wes said. I smiled widely and looked up at her. She wore an expression I couldn't quite read.

"Thank you," I said. Everly was a beautiful girl, and if I truly did look anything like her, I was a lucky girl.

"Well, we should go. I just wanted to make sure you had your things," she said.

"Thank you so much." My chest tightened, and I felt like I was losing my chance again. Like they were slipping through my fingers, and there was nothing I could do about it.

"Dear, I called the police Academy, and they said they would pass the message to him," Judy said in the doorway. My heart sank. The quickest Easton would be here would be an hour, and that was if he hit most of the green lights. Everly took Wes's hand and tried to pull him off the bed, but he wouldn't budge.

"Nooo," he whined.

"Wes, don't do this. We have to go."

I swallowed down the uncertainty surrounding what I was about to do and just did it. "Stay?"

"What?" Everly asked.

"Yeah!" Wes cheered.

"Please stay. My husband is a least an hour out. I have

nobody here with me. I'm scared. Can you stay? At least until he gets here?" I asked, my voice tapering off as another contraction came. "Ahhh!"

"OK. OK. OK. We'll stay!" Everly took my hand in hers and squeezed it tight. The electric shock ran up my arm.

CHAPTER 19

*E*verly gripped my hand tight as the contractions wracked through my body. I was practically begging for the epidural by the time it was first offered to me, and I accepted before Judy could even finish talking. Everly held my hand for that too and I stared into her beautiful green eyes—my eyes—as the needle penetrated deep into my spine. Sweat dripped from my hairline and my heart pounded in my chest. My body felt as if it were under attack from the inside out, and my heart felt guarded but full. The last thing I wanted was to scare my niece, and I worried Chloe would walk through the door at any moment. Or worse, my brother.

Having my niece and nephew with me was my chance to tell them everything I had ever wanted. But I couldn't do that with words. I couldn't tell them what I wanted to; the stories of their dad when he was a little boy or what it was like to grow up with their grandma and grandpa. I couldn't tell them that one day—when I was truly gone—I'd watch out over them. Or that I had been doing it now. I'd have to convey the love I had for them in another way. "Tell me about yourself," I said to Everly as the epidural worked its magic and blocked out the pain.

"Well, I'm graduating high school soon, and I'm going to be a graphic artist," Everly said. Her cheeks were red, just like mine had been my whole life. *Lives.*

"Oh, wow. Is that something that runs in the family?" I prodded.

"Actually, yeah. My aunt was going to be a graphic artist too. The talent skipped my dad, but my grandma has it even though she says she doesn't." Everly tucked her ashy blond strands behind her ears and then returned her clasped hands to her lap. She was nervous.

I thought about all the terrible drawings Carter drew as a kid. "Your aunt?" *What was I doing?*

"Oh, yeah. Sorry, she died," Everly waved her hand dismissively.

My gut wrenched, though not from a contraction. Or if it was, I guess I wouldn't have known, as I was numb from the waist down. But there was something to be said about listening to your own bloodline talk about how you died. Especially when they batted their hand as if it were an annoyance. I couldn't blame her, though. The girl had never met me. My brother wasn't much of a talker, so I assumed he hadn't opened up much to anyone about me. She probably heard some stories from my parents now and then growing up, but that still didn't make me real to her. Or important. But if she knew it was me here now, that would change things. . .

"Oh no! I'm so sorry," I said. I was sorry I couldn't stay longer to have met her.

"Oh, it's OK. It was a long time ago," she said.

"Yeah, but . . . I'm sure it's really hard?"

"Um . . . well, like I didn't know her. So. . ." Everly shrugged. *I deserved that.* I had no right trying to dig into her past, *my past . . .*

"Right." I stared at her, searching for hidden feelings deep down inside while she looked around the hospital room nervously.

"Actually, you kind of look like her," she said. A smile tugged at the corners of my mouth. It wasn't much, but at least there was that. And the art; that was special too.

"Look who's talking," I laughed, caught up in the moment. It wasn't until her eyebrows pulled that I realized I had said too much. "Oh, wow. Is it hot in here? It's so hot." I placed the back of my palm against my forehead, and Everly jumped up to feel if I had a fever.

"Should I call the nurse?" she asked.

"No, I think I'm OK. But thank you. So, tell me about Car . . . Your dad . . ." *Shit . . .*

"My dad? He just works. Like all the time. That's it," she shrugged again.

"Hu . . . And your mom?"

"My mom's busy with this little guy—" Everly motioned to Wes sitting on a chair with her cell phone. "He was an oops baby. He's the apple of her eye, though," she said with a smile. I felt bad for her. The poor girl needed her aunt, and I wasn't there for her.

"And you?" I asked.

"I had my time when I was a baby. I had been the only grandkid for many years."

"Huh. . ." I rubbed my belly, never wanting either of the twins to feel like they were second best.

"I have a boyfriend. . ." she said.

"You do?"

"Yeah. We've been dating for a little over a year now. I'm not sure what we're going to do when he moves away to college. I guess we're going to try and make it work. But, it'll be hard. I'm staying local. There's a great university nearby for the arts," Everly said while looking down at her feet, a helpless fog in her eyes.

"Try not to dwell on it. I think everything will work out just the way it's supposed to," I said.

"You think?"

"I know," I said.

It was then that I caught a figure standing in the doorway. Easton. He sprinted into the room and wrapped his arms around me tight. "I'm so sorry. I came as fast as I could. I got a police escort," Easton said, his face buried in my neck.

"It's OK. I've been in good company," I said.

Easton pulled away and stilled for a moment as he looked into my eyes, surveying them. He straightened his back and turned to Everly. "Hello," he said, tight-lipped.

"Hi. Um, I'm Everly, and that's my little brother, Wes. We were just leaving," Everly said, standing.

"Hi buddy," Easton said to Wes.

"Hi."

"Lucky for me, Everly and Wes were at the park when

my water broke. They drove me here and have been keeping me company while I've been waiting for you," I said.

"You've been a big help today. Thank you, buddy," Easton said to Wes.

"Yeah. With my sisers. . ." Wes said.

Easton stared at the little boy as he mindlessly played on the phone. Everly shook her head, dismissively rolling her eyes at his comment. Easton's eyes flickered to mine, and the air shifted in the room. Frigid goosebumps prickled my skin.

"OK, well. We better go. I wish you and your baby the best," Everly said.

"Babies. There's two of them," I told her.

"Wow. That's . . . Wow." Everly shook her head. "Come on, little man. Time to say goodbye."

"Bye. Bye. Bye sissser. Bye," Wes waived on his way out the door.

"Bye, buddy. Bye!" I blew a kiss, and the last thing I saw before the door closed was his chubby cheeks pucker into a smile. The moment they were gone, a weight had lifted off my chest that I didn't even know I'd been carrying. I took a deep breath for the first time since my labor had started and turned my gaze to Easton. Who was . . . not happy.

"What?"

"What in the world was that?" he demanded.

"Oh. That. Well, I was at the park—"

"The park?"

I closed my eyes for a moment of regret. The labor had

somehow made my lips loose, and I had been divulging too much. "I sometimes . . . go to the park to read, and—"

"You mean the park next to your brother's house?"

"Well . . . that's the only one around. So—"

"Beck, what are you doing?"

"I'm sorry! I'm sorry, I just . . ."

"You're not sorry."

He called my bluff. "I'm not sorry," I admitted, picking at an imaginary fuzz on my hospital blanket. "I sometimes go just to watch Wes play. And Chloe is such a good mom. It's just . . . I don't know . . . It's nice. It's nice to see that the life I left behind was still going, and that I didn't disrupt it too much by leaving. I like seeing them happy. It makes me feel whole," I said, shrugging. I wasn't sorry for making my heart full. It was essential to my well-being.

"That's fair," Easton admitted. His tone heavy with sadness. "Have you ever been caught?"

"No! No . . . But this one time, Wes called me his sister. And then I hid behind a book."

"Sister?"

"Yeah. I think he senses that she and I are alike." I nodded, keeping the part where I voluntarily lifted my disguise, winked at the boy, and probably gave him nightmares.

"So, how did they end up here?" Easton asked, sitting on the bed.

"Well, my water broke—"

"While you were stalking your past life at the park?"

"Yes . . ." A moment of silence stretched between us.

"And your niece happened to?"

"Well, I couldn't drive. Brooklyn had just left, and Everly was the only one there. So, she drove me."

"Brooklyn?"

"Yeah. . ."

"Uh-huh." Easton sighed. I knew I pushed the limits of what he'd been comfortable with. Being a Tethered Soul came with rules, and I didn't follow any of them. But it wasn't an opportunity I could waste.

"Sorry," I said. "I don't want to make you worry."

Easton leaned over me and tucked my hair behind my ear. "You don't need to apologize for wanting to see your family happy." I nodded. Tears pricked my eyes, and my chin wobbled. It's all I really wanted. For them to be happy.

Easton and I chatted until the wee hours of the night when my monitors went haywire. Nurses rushed to my room, checking me and the machines I was hooked up to. I watched them frantically, trying to read their faces.

"Is everything OK?" Easton asked.

Everything happened so fast, it was a whirlwind of nurses and alarms. Panic set deep within the eyes of those who surrounded me. My hand slipped out of Easton's as I was wheeled off to an emergency C-section. I felt my tether pull tight as our distance stretched, and I knew he felt the same.

The room I entered for surgery was eerie and my instincts told me I should run. This was not how I had planned my delivery, and I knew I was in trouble. Panic had set in, my breathing shallow and erratic as a nurse placed an oxygen mask over my head. With large gulps of air, I watched my doctor wash up through a window. Even his eyes were unnerving.

A curtain went up at my chest, separating my line of sight from my stomach. And though I couldn't feel myself being sliced open, my body shook with the tugging of my flesh. I tried to be brave. I tried to keep calm. But I had a sense of fear that came from deep down inside that I couldn't seem to shake. I closed my eyes, steadying my breath, and when I felt brave enough, I opened them and tried to read the expression of the surrounding staff. It was something in the way that Judy looked that told me I'd be able to read her face like a book. I kept my eyes on hers, my heart nearly stopping until the slightest curve of her lips appeared. And then there was a small, distant cry from beyond the sheet.

"It's a girl!" Dr. Faye announced.

I sobbed as the room erupted into claps and cheers of congratulations. My emotions were scattered like a bag of dropped marbles. I felt everything. And when they showed me her pink little wrinkled body, I saw everything I had felt for her, floating in the air. Surrounding us all. Little bits of glowing lights with the warmth of happiness and hope. It was like a meteor shower inside the hospital, and it struck me with wonder, leaving me in awe. I knew I would give anything or be anything for that little girl the moment I laid eyes on her. And giving up eternal life for her was the most honorable thing I could ever do.

I tried to control my sobbing long enough to ask for the nurses to tell Easton, but the tears just kept coming, with no end in sight. They took my little girl away, and I kept busy by watching the stars twinkle softy. Yellow sparkles glowed brightly until something changed.

At first, the brightness had dimmed, leaving the room a darker shade of love and hope. Then it was the warmth that dissipated, turning the room chilly and bitter. My body trembled, twitching and jerking on top of the table. I watched the magic turn blood red before disappearing into thin wisps of smoke, and I was left with the devastation of what I had not yet known but felt in my heart. I swallowed down the rising bile in my throat and lowered my gaze slowly. The staff was silent. Judy would not look at me.

Dr. Faye came to my side and picked up my hand. Before he had the chance to say anything at all, a deep guttural cry ripped through me. "I'm so sorry," he said. The staff stilled, and time stopped. The only thing I could feel was pain. Pain so sharp that I could barely catch my breath. I was being suffocated with the truth of losing a child, and I was going to die right here on this table of a broken, battered heart. I don't know how long I cried for, and I'm not sure how long I lay in the darkness of a room that was once lit with love, but I knew one thing; I'd never come back from this.

CHAPTER 20

When I was lucid enough to understand that this was real life and not some terrible night terror, I was completely gutted. It wasn't just that I no longer shared my body with two babies or that my legs were still numb. It was that my emotions were gone, too. All but one. Devastation. And there was so much of it that I felt hallow inside. I couldn't see the love floating in the air, and I couldn't feel it swell in my chest. I wasn't sure I ever would again. I stared unfocused into the middle of the room as Easton stroked my hair. All I could do was blink because even acknowledging his presence was too difficult for me.

It wasn't until the nurse brought our baby girl into the room that I felt like the worst mother there had ever been. Because even she made me feel nothing. Easton tried to get me to engage, but I just stared at the wall. My mind telling me I was useless. A mother who couldn't protect her child. I never even had the chance. I never got to hold it, and they never felt my love. I failed. My one job, my one purpose in this life, and I failed. How could I live with myself now?

I closed my eyes and rubbed where the crust had formed from countless dried tears. Inevitably I would have to live with myself because now, I'd be living forever. There was no way I could live a fulfilling life now that I had lost a child. Easton was right, after all. This was a tortured life. I could see it now, and I could feel it right about where my heart used to be. I would have to ask him if he saw the burning rings of smoldering ember radiating off me like he had seen with other tortured souls.

The baby cried, and Easton sang a lullaby as he walked her around the room. I was so thankful for his strength to carry on when I couldn't. I didn't know how, but I knew I must find a way to be there for my little girl. Even through the pain and the fog of failure. I was still a mother to one, and I had to be strong enough to be there for her. I opened my eyes. It was the first step. I blinked several times, and I made myself a promise.

You can do this, Beck. You can do this. If you can show up for that little girl, be the mother she needs, I promise . . . you can fall to pieces every other waking second. But for her, you must not give up.

I rolled onto my back, giving it everything I had, and focused my eyes on Easton.

"Hey, there she is. . ." Easton came to me, and I sat up in the hospital bed. "I think she's hungry. You've been . . . out for a while." Easton handed me the wrapped little peanut, and I reached out instinctively to take her. I had hoped that when I took her in my arms, something would change. My heart would light fire again, and I would come back for her. But it didn't, and I was no phoenix. I looked at her little red face, and all I could think was how will I ever love her with a broken heart?

I looked up to Easton, the worry etched deep into my face, and I could see that he understood without having to say it. His eyes watered, and he nodded at me. "It's going to be OK. We're going to get through this," he said in a whisper. I'm not sure why it hurt to hear it. Maybe it was because everything hurt? Maybe because I didn't think it was true. Or maybe I knew one day we would get through it, and that hurt too. I didn't want my child to be something that I one day moved on from. And I didn't think that the doom would ever subside or that my heart would ever be whole again.

"Let's name her Clara," Easton said. I looked up at him. His eyes sad, but there, just on the edges, was a touch of hope.

"Clara. . ."

The time I spent at the hospital went by in a fog. I assume some of that was due to the pain medication, and if I hadn't known any better, I'd say they gave me a little extra to help get me past the first few days after the stillbirth. I slept a lot in the hospital, but even when I was awake, a part of me still lingered somewhere in far-off land. Easton and I had to name our other daughter, but I found it incredibly difficult to give her a name that she'd never use. I wondered if it would hurt more or help with closure. Either way, Easton said she deserved a beautiful name, and I couldn't argue with that.

"What about Molly?" I asked him. He rocked Clara in his arms as we waited to be discharged from the hospital.

"Molly and Clara, I like it," he said. I nodded and then looked away. Molly would forever be the name I associated with the deepest sorrow and the blood-painted smoke in the operation room.

Nurse Judy came in to give us some paperwork. Easton handed me Clara so that he could fill it out. I took her warm little wrapped body in my arms and stroked her forehead with my fingertips.

"Do you have the names yet?" she asked.

"Molly and Clara Green," Easton smiled.

"Those are lovely names. Just keep filling that out. I'm going to get a wheelchair for you, Miss Becca, and a little something someone dropped off for you today," Judy said before disappearing from the room.

"Thank you," I said, not in the least curious what it was or who it came from. When she returned with a small brown teddy bear, I forced a polite smile.

"Here you are. A pretty little girl dropped that off today. Your sister? She looked just like you," the nurse said.

My eyes grew, and I reached for the tag. The instant I saw 'Congratulations,' my stomach churned. It wasn't a good feeling to be told congratulations when a tragedy had just happened. I knew I needed to separate the death from the birth. If I hadn't, poor Clara would forever live in the shadow of Molly's tragedy, and that was no way to raise a child. But I didn't know how to compartmentalize the two. I flipped the tag over to see Everly's name, and it sparked an ember in my broken heart. I'd have to keep this bear safe, and one day, I would explain to Clara just how important it was.

Judy helped me to the wheelchair, and we eventually left the hospital. A part of me didn't want to leave because inside these walls, I was once a mother of two. Somehow, leaving the hospital made it more real, and the reality sank in that I would be going home with only one of my children. When the cold air met my face, I breathed in my new life with the fresh winter air—and reluctantly—I exhaled the old one out. Molly overshadowed all the bits of excitement that I once had to be a mother, and I felt no joy to begin my journey.

Brooklyn and Tanner were waiting for us when we got home. And if that wasn't hard enough to see them, I still had to come home to the house that was prepped for two babies. Brooklyn had expected that, and she and Tanner worked tirelessly removing the second crib, second swing, second . . . everything. There was no evidence whatsoever that I had planned for twins. Not in the closet, not in the drawers, and not on the walls. I was relieved that I didn't have to come home and see it all. But there was also a part of me that hated seeing it gone, and I knew that was the part of me that simply wasn't ready to let go. I wondered if that part would live in me forever.

During this troublesome time, the nights were especially grueling because that's when Clara would stay up crying. And to be honest, it was in the off hours she slept that I would keep my promise to myself. When the house was quiet and all were asleep, I'd slip into the garage, climb inside my truck and shut the door tight behind me. I'd grip the steering wheel and listen to the hum of silence for a few seconds before I'd cry. It happened nightly at first. And when I cried myself to sleep in my truck, Easton just about had a heart attack looking for me. After I'd confessed to my promise and my nightly belligerent sessions, he would often check on me in the garage if I wasn't in bed. Countless nights he crawled inside the cab with me and held me till my tears ran dry. Sometimes, he'd cry too.

But when Clara was up, that was my time to give her what she deserved. A stable, loving mother. And I loved her right. That was the easy part. The hard part was being stable. I had a good streak going, but I told myself it was OK for all the times I failed and broke down in front of her. She wouldn't remember them, anyway. No, I had a good five years of mistakes before she really remembered what I was like as a mother, and for that, I was thankful.

The shadow that Molly cast on Clara was short-lived. About six weeks after she was born, when I walked into the nursery, Clara smiled at me. It nearly brought me to my knees to see her acknowledge me, and I felt my heart stitch back together. Until then, it had felt like a thankless job, but the moment she smiled at me, I knew it was neither of those things. In the days that followed, I spent my time trying to get her to do it again and then again. Hungry for her little toothless grin because somehow it was the glue that mended my heart back together, and it was Clara who taught me how to love again.

It wasn't long after the smile had renewed my sense of hope that I could hike a trail—albeit slowly—and that is what I was waiting on for Molly's ceremony. I wanted to spread her ashes over the Truly River where Easton and I married in my first life and where we were engaged for my second one. It was a meaningful spot to me, full of memories. And I wanted my Molly to rest in the field where I saw the shape of love for the first time. My parents came, too, and so did Easton's. Brooklyn and Tanner joined as well, completing our family. It was difficult having all the people around, but I was glad they came. And after six weeks, I had finally gathered the strength to face the day I'd say goodbye.

After a slow hike down the trail, we reached the vast opening in the field. It was weird to show up with other people as it had always been a secret spot for Easton and me. Even the day we wed was unconventional. It had just been the two of us. But this felt right, and her memorial was similar in how it too was unconventional. I ran my hands across the tall wet blades of grass and marveled at the beauty beyond the cliffs. My dress soaked up the winter dew much like it had before—and even though we were saying goodbye and my dress was now black—I couldn't help but feel like I had been here before.

The family gathered at the cliff's edge. Easton held my hand and his mother held Clara. A crisp breeze passed by, and I thought it was odd how I hadn't felt the chill, just air that had passed through my hair.

"The most beautiful things on this green earth cannot be seen but must be felt. Molly has touched our hearts, and though she may be gone, she will not be forgotten," Easton spoke softly. I felt a gentle pull in my attention. Like eyes had been watching me from behind. I turned my head, the breeze dancing in my hair. A dragonfly buzzed across the field, lighting it up with love.

Easton let go of my hand to open the urn. I turned around to watch my daughter fly, but all I saw was ash. Black lifeless particles that painted the sky before dispersing into nothing. Molly had not been inside that urn. As everyone cried and embraced, I turned my head back around to the sparkling field and imagined my Molly chasing the dragonflies.

CHAPTER 21

The ceremony marked the beginning of a new chapter for me. The one where I became a mother. Of course, I had been a mother for the six weeks prior, but it wasn't until I saw the ash flutter down in the chilly winter air that I realized it wasn't my Molly. No, Molly was in the fields chasing the twinkling lights. Basking in love that sprinkled between the blades of grass and twirled through the breeze. I didn't say goodbye that day, but I did embrace my present life. And I no longer looked at Clara as a reminder of what I'd lost. It was a hard place in my broken heart to find, but once I found the part that could both love and mourn—side by side—I became a better version of myself. Certainly, a stronger one.

The nights were still difficult, and most days, I felt like a zombie, but Easton was marvelous at picking up the pieces that I either dropped or no longer could carry. When he and Tanner graduated from the police academy, I knew our lives would take yet another turn. I was happy for him, but it didn't make the long hours any less lonely. Easton always said that he wanted to make an honest living, and with a family by his side, he said it was finally time. On the other hand, I was perfectly fine making ends meet in any which way he knew how. I hadn't married him to change him after all. I married him because I couldn't live without him. And some days, it felt like I was.

I'm sure it was hard for anyone to put their life on hold to raise a child. But when you knew that your life would never end, it's a different kind of hard. Don't get me wrong, I wouldn't give it up for the world. *I wouldn't.* But I just wished Clara would talk or *something.* Some days I would get so sick of hearing my voice I'd have to turn on the music to drown myself out. Or worse, call my mother. Sometimes she would come stay with us, and normally that would be too much for me, but now I welcomed the company. I needed to be seen and heard. My mom did that for me, and after some time, we became friends in a way we never had before. She talked about the divorce a lot, and I talked about losing my identity. It seems we both didn't know who we were anymore, and simply knowing that I wasn't alone made me feel better.

A new pastime of mine had become watching the neighbors. I had three particularly sneaky spots around the house that I would spy from; the front window, the mailbox —which had a better view down the street—and the backyard. However, the backyard was better suited for listening. The old lady down the street—I named her Nancy —went missing for a week. When she finally returned, she was in a wheelchair. I think it was a heart issue, but Easton has his money on a stroke. And the neighbors next door fight all the time. He hides the fact that he smokes cigarettes, and he usually sneaks out back after they fight for a nicotine fix.

The neighbors weren't my friends, but they were a nice supplement to keep my mind busy. Of course, Brooklyn was still my best friend several years later, but she and Tanner had become quite serious, and they started spending more time by themselves. They announced they would move in together on Clara's second birthday. I tried to help her move, but Clara made more of a mess than I could help pack and ultimately, we had to leave early so Brooklyn could get proper work done. More often than not, I felt more of a burden than a friend, and I longed for the days when she enjoyed my company again.

I'd be seeing her today though, for a summer wrap-up barbeque I was hosting, and I couldn't be more excited to get the time to talk with her.

Brooklyn came over early to help me set up. It was a small gathering, only Tanner, Brooklyn, and a family down the street with a little boy Clara's age. They were just far enough I couldn't spy on them, which made them appear seemingly normal. They were also the only family around with kids.

"Do you think this is enough silverware?" Brooklyn asked.

"Yeah, for sure. Thanks for helping," I said.

"Anytime! Is Clara's boyfriend coming today?"

"Jackson isn't her boyfriend. They barely even notice each other. It's kind of weird."

"Then why are they coming?" Brooklyn asked. It was a fair question; why would I invite a family with a kid that my kid hadn't even taken notice of. I guess I just felt that she should have a friend come, and since she didn't have friends yet, the little boy would have to do.

"Um, it's for social skills. She's going to start kindergarten next week, and I can't have her unsocialized," I said, shrugging.

"Huh. I just think the parents are super awkward."

"Oh my god, tell me about it! The last time they were over—"

"Wow. Is that for me?" Clara screeched. I spun around to see her standing in her pajamas, clutching her stuffed elephant. "Brooklyn brought that cake for everybody. Doesn't it look good?" I scooped Clara up in my arms, and she smiled a toothy grin.

"It's a party!" she squirmed. I put her down, and she ran to the appetizers.

"You woke up from your nap just in time. The party is about to start. Let's get you changed," I said, taking Clara back to her bedroom. Tanner walked in the front door as I passed, and he gave me a quick kiss on the cheek hello. "Hi, I think Easton is out back setting up the food." I waved to the backyard, but Tanner wasn't looking for his brother. His eyes fell upon Brooklyn.

I was almost finished with Clara's hair when Easton popped into her room. "Wow, you look so pretty. Are you ready for the barbecue? Everybody is here," Easton said. Clara jumped up and down.

"Hold on. Hold still," I said, tying the last bow in her

hair before she sprinted out of the room and down the hall. I sighed, looking up at Easton, and he came to my side and rubbed my shoulders. "Oh, that feels so good." I rolled my head from side to side. Easton leaned down to my ear and whispered.

"I have a secret. . ."

I perked up. Secrets were scarce these days. "What? Tell me."

"Can you keep it?" Easton teased.

I looked back to Clara's open door. "Yeah, you know I can. What is it?"

"Tanner is going to ask Brooklyn to marry him," Easton whispered.

"What?" My jaw unhinged, hanging low and open.

"Shhh."

"When?"

"Today, if all goes well," he said, just before walking out of Clara's room. I lingered for a moment, worrying that Tanner would get his heart broken. He didn't know Brooklyn like we did. She was a true free spirit, and I feared she looked at marriage like a ball and chain around her ankle. At least she had before she fell in love with Tanner.

The barbecue went well. Clara and Jackson played together for the first time. And the neighbors kept a good flow of conversation without doing that thing they always did that made Brooklyn and me think they were so awkward to be around. I knew an end of summer barbeque wasn't a romantic setting—not in the least—but the day was next to perfect, and it was amongst the people we cared about most . . . and the neighbors. I knew Tanner would propose soon, and it made me anxious.

When the neighbors had left, and Clara was crazed under the influence of sugar, Tanner took Brooklyn aside. My eyes shot to Easton's, and then we both ran to the master bathroom that had a window opened to the backyard. It was perfect, but only one of us could see at a time, and it wasn't much. Only a sliver of kneecaps could be seen through the slats of the window. But we could both hear crystal clear, and we pressed our ears close to the open window.

"Today was fun," Tanner started.

"It was fun. Clara loved the dessert."

"I really enjoy spending time over here with my brother and his family."

"Yeah. Me too."

"Think that could be us one day?" Tanner asked. I grinned and popped my head up to look through the vented window. He was holding her hands. I panned to his face; he looked pale.

"He's so nervous," I whispered. Easton raised his head to look, and I moved out of his way.

"You want kids?" Brooklyn asked. My breath stilled as I looked at Easton. He had no idea what kept a Tethered Soul bound, and after all these years, I had no intention of telling him.

"I want kids with you. I want a family with you. I want to spend the rest of my life with you. I love you. And if you would let me, I'd—" Tanner lowered down to his knee. Easton and I fought over the small window, our temples competing for headspace.

"Stop!" Brooklyn said.

"Oh, no," I whispered.

"Tanner, I can't have you do this."

"Do what?"

"I can't have you get down on one knee for me."

"I can't see!" I hissed.

"I can't either," Easton replied.

"I can't have you ask for my hand in marriage. . ."

"What's that?" Clara squawked, startling both Easton and me.

"Nothing! There's a bug," I whispered to Clara.

"Can I see?" she asked, her voice much louder than ours. Easton and I ducked below the window, hoping not to get caught.

"Yes. Your dad will show you the bug from the outside. Go show her, honey," I said. Easton glared at me for a split second before turning to Clara with a smile.

"You want to see some bugs? I'll show you some bugs!" He picked her up and took her out of the bathroom. I stood on my tippy toes, pressing my cheek against the window sill. Brooklyn was gone, and Tanner was left staring at the ring in his hands. My stomach dropped. I knew why Brooklyn did it, but I wish she hadn't. I set out to find her. I made it just in time to see her car backing out of the driveway. I ran outside and prompted her to stop.

"Brooklyn, are you OK?" I asked. Tears streamed down her face. It was a stupid question.

"I can't talk right now, Becca."

"I know what happened. I'm so sorry."

Brooklyn threw her car in park and looked up, blinking back the tears. "I can't marry him, Bec," she confessed.

I sighed. If only she knew she had a choice. "I know," I said.

"I gotta get out of here."

"Hey, I think Clara is just going to nap, and Easton can watch her. Do you want some company?" I asked. Brooklyn nodded. I took a moment to run inside and tell Easton and gather my things. When I hopped in her car, her tears had stopped and her face held a vacant expression. We drove around for a little while until Brooklyn stopped at the park. It was the place I found myself often, and the times she had accompanied me were the times we usually had our deeper conversations. Perhaps it was because Clara had entertained herself in the sandbox.

As we walked through the grass to the benches, I watched a dad play with his little girl. She appeared to be Clara's age, and I tried to hide my excitement that she may have a potential new friend.

"The hard part is that I love him. I don't want to break up with him. But it's not like I can stay with him now that he knows I don't want to get married and have kids . . . No offense," Brooklyn said. I frowned for a second, showing my true colors before playing it off.

"None taken."

"I mean, I knew I shouldn't have gotten as close as I allowed myself to get. It's my fault. I deserve this."

"You deserve to be happy, Brooklyn," I said, watching the man push his daughter on the swings. He looked oddly familiar.

"I am happy. Not in this exact moment, but in general. I'm a free spirit. I'm a wanderer. And I wouldn't have it any other way. Love just ties you down . . . No offense." We sat down on the bench, and I placed my bag to my side. I thought about love tying me down, but it wasn't like that for Easton and me. Quite the opposite, really. Easton's love was the one thing that saved me from myself. If I had a tether holding me back, it would have to be *me*. I'm not sure I'd know how to survive without him.

"It's survival of the fittest, Becca. And I need to shake it off if I want to survive. So that's it. I'm done with relationships. Forever."

"Oh my god . . . I think that's my OB-GYN," I said, squinting.

Brooklyn raised her brows, not at all minding the interruption. "Damn, he's hot!" she said. I said nothing, but my head nodded ever so slightly. "And he was the one who gave you all of those exams?" she asked. My cheeks flushed, and my head continued to bob slowly until our eyes met, and we began to laugh.

CHAPTER 22

My hand clung to Clara's as I walked her into kindergarten. Miss Kay's classroom was bright and colorful, and it smelled of crayons and glue. Most of the parents hung around the outskirts of the classroom while one gave their crying son a private pep talk in the corner. I was anxious. I could only imagine what Clara was feeling.

"OK, honey, you need to go sit on the rug. I'm going to stay for a little, but then I'll have to go home so you can learn," I said, kneeling down on one knee.

Clara smiled, her blond hair sticking to her cheeks as I tucked it behind her ears. "OK, mommy." She kissed me before turning to join the other kids. She found her way to the middle of the rug and sat down next to a little girl with long, dark hair. I tried to be happy for her, but I couldn't help but feel like she left just a little too, easy. She never even looked back. Not once. I frowned, looking back to the kid who refused to leave the comfort of his mother.

"How are you holding up?" a dad asked beside me. I looked up at his tall stature, and my stomach dropped. It was my doctor. The same one from the park the week prior and the same one from the exam room. My cheeks heated with embarrassment. Had I felt exposed? This man knew way too much. He'd *seen* way too much. And he'd been there in my darkest hour. . .

"Dr. Faye, so nice to see you again."

"I thought I recognized you. Remind me—"

"Becca Green. You delivered Clara—" I motioned toward the middle of the rug and then wrapped my hand around the nape of my neck and spoke a little softer, "and Molly . . ."

"That's right," he said. I hated how the mood shifted after I said it, but pretending she never existed was far worse. It was something I'd have to get used to, though five years later, and it still hurt. I wasn't sure it would ever change.

"I thought I saw you last week at the park just down the street. Did you just move here or something?" I asked.

"Yes, actually we did. We moved about a month ago. We wanted little Nora to be close to her school so that she could join after-school programs. We thought it might be easier for her to make friends if she wasn't so far away."

I nodded, looking back to Clara. "Is she yours? With the long dark hair?" I asked.

"Yes, and that's . . . ?" he pointed to Clara.

"Yes! That's Clara. Looks like they've already become friends," I said, watching the girls giggle. I'd never seen Clara so chatty, and I assumed it was because the only other friend she had was the boy who lived down the street. I didn't like boys until I had met Easton. I thought back to the day I met him, when I was eight. It was weird to think that Clara could meet her husband in just three years.

"Well, that makes me feel better knowing Nora has a friend," Dr. Faye said.

"Yeah, me too. I can leave knowing she's not alone today," I said with a smile. And while Clara wouldn't be alone on her first day of kindergarten, I would be alone for the first time in years. I did what any mom would do with her day off. I went home and cried. Actually, I didn't quite make it home; I cried in my truck while sitting in the parking lot. And when I arrived home to an empty house, I cried a little more, but mostly I busied myself with cleaning the house. I checked my watch about a million times, worried I'd be late for pick up and Clara would be afraid. I kept imagining her crying on the sidewalk all alone, and it made my stomach churn. If I had learned anything about myself by now, it was that I didn't deal with life transitions all that well. Six weeks, I told myself. Six weeks until this was the new normal.

I checked my watch again and realized it had only been two hours. I threw the sponge in the sink and ran a hand through my hair. There was something about Dr. Faye knowing about Molly that made it impossible not to feel the raw emotions all over again. It seemed like it was yesterday I was lying in that bed, unable to feel my body and watching the room turn. The glowing shimmer of light bleeding away into dark burgundy. I could still feel the chill in the room on my arms and down my back, even now as I stood at the sink some five years later.

I remembered the girl in the field that day we said goodbye to Molly. A little toe head catching the sparks of magic. I wondered what it would be like to look in the backyard now and see two little girls instead of just one. Was it possible it was the reason Clara didn't play with other children? Had she felt it deep down inside that she lost her twin? Was she lonely?

Easton and I had decided to tell Clara about Molly when she was young. Young enough not to understand. And ever since then, we talked about her here and there. 'Your sister Molly would have loved this, something simple as a reminder that she did, in fact, have a twin. I never wanted her to grow up and realize that we kept it from her. I had held on to too many secrets in my time, and I chose for this not to be one of them.

Clara never said much about her sister. Not after that phase passed. But there was a time when Clara would talk to Molly and "play" with her in the backyard. There was always a part of me that wondered if it was really her. Had she come back to play with her sister? She wasn't the typical imaginary friend, after all. A piece of me knew deep down in my heart that I didn't really believe it but that I just didn't want to let her go. It was my way of holding onto hope that Molly was somehow OK. I later realized that if you want something bad enough, your mind will bend in ways it shouldn't. Connecting pieces of the puzzle that really didn't fit in the first place, but if pressed hard enough may appear to work. And I knew that was the case now when I considered if Clara's new friend at school was something more. I knew it was simply my mind playing tricks on me. But as soon as I thought it, I couldn't shake it. What if that little girl had Molly's soul?

I had only seen the little girl's face for a fraction of a second, and what I gathered, she looked just like her father. He was ruggedly handsome, with bright blue eyes. His hair, though grey now, was most likely dark when he was younger. But why had Clara taken to the little girl so effortlessly? Typically, she was a shy girl. She didn't like other kids, and she had only played with Jackson once in all the years they had lived down the street. I knew it was me unable to let go of Molly. I knew it was seeing Dr. Faye and the old feelings resurfacing that made me dig deep for anything I could grasp onto. And I knew the silence in the house wasn't helping either. But what had stopped Molly from being a Tethered Soul? And if it were genetic, wouldn't both girls be tethered? Molly could be out there somewhere.

It wasn't . . . *impossible.*

By the time I got to school, I was an hour early. I simply couldn't take the waiting any longer. And my mind had been playing mean, mean tricks on me. A rush of adrenaline coursing through my veins told me this was a very dangerous mindset for me to be in. This wasn't as simple as spying on the neighbors. This was a family. A good family. And this was my daughter, the one I'd never met. The one who died. *God, Beck, get it together!*

I gripped my steering wheel, barely holding on to my sanity when Miss Kay's class walked single file before my truck. I sat up tall in my seat and lowered my sunglasses to the bridge of my nose. I peered down the line of kids until I found Clara. Her hand behind her as she held on to Nora's little fingers. My stomach dropped. *See?* They had the same figure. Same stature. They looked . . . similar. Fair skin, chubby cheeks. Nora had dark hair, and Clara was a toe-head . . . But that meant nothing. The fact that they were holding hands *did*, though. They had a bond. But was it a sisterly bond? That was the question. I watched until the class disappeared into the room, and then I had the idea of a lifetime. I lept out of my truck and marched to the front office.

"Hi. I'm a parent of one of the kids in Miss Kay's class, and I wanted to sign up to volunteer," I smiled at the lady behind the front desk.

"I'm sorry, but we don't allow volunteers the first quarter," she said.

"I'm sorry—what?"

"We don't allow volunteers," she repeated.

"You don't *allow* . . . free help?"

"Not for the first quarter, no. It's harder on the little ones when the parents are hanging around. After the teachers establish a routine, and all the kids are used to being dropped off, then we open volunteer enrollment."

I stared at her for a long awkward moment. It was the stupidest rule I'd ever heard. "So I can't sign up?"

"No, ma'am. Not until quarter two. And that's if you make the list."

"The list? I might not make it now?" I asked.

"Many of the parents want to volunteer, and there are

only so many spots we can offer before it's a distraction for the kids."

"Can I sign up now?"

"I'm sorry. You'll have to wait until the sign-up e-mail gets sent out," she said. I sighed and checked my watch. I still had ten minutes before Clara got out.

"OK. Thanks," I said, deflated. So much for my brilliant plan. I'd have to find another way to spy on the little girl. *Oh god.* Could I hear myself? Was I going crazy? Was this how my life turns out? I wind up with a restraining order from a five-year-old? And did she really call me ma'am?

Dr. Faye walked up to me as I stood on the curb contemplating my bright future. "You couldn't wait either?" he asked.

I smiled, my eyes wide with alarm. If only he knew what I had been plotting. "I was anxious, I guess," I said. That much was true.

"Yeah, me too."

"Where is Nora's mom?" I asked absentmindedly. "Oh my god. That was really rude of me to assume. . ." I said, searching his face and wishing I could take it back.

"No, it's alright. My wife and I work at the hospital, so our hours are atypical."

"Oh, yeah. Right. Well, I know you just moved here, and our daughters seemed to hit it off, so if you want to get them together at the park, that would be fun. . ." I shrugged. The class let out, and the kids were released one at a time. I watched, waiting for Clara, hoping that she would wear a giant smile on her face. And I may or may not have been looking for Nora, too.

"That would be wonderful. Do you still have my number?" Dr. Faye asked.

"Huh?"

"My emergency number, it's my cell phone."

"Oh, no. I don't have it anymore." I said. Because that would be weird if I hung on to it.

"Let me give it to you then," he said.

I pulled out my phone and typed his name in. When his contact came up with both office and personal cell phone numbers, I pretended to enter it all over again. Clara ran up to me during the last two digits and slammed into my legs.

"Mommy!" she screeched. I kneeled, giving her a tight hug. It was only my first day alone in the house, but I missed her much more than I expected. As I grasped my daughter tight, Nora came up behind her back, and our eyes met for the first time. If I hadn't known any better, I'd think my heart stopped beating for one breathless moment. She was stunning. Her blue eyes, her dark hair, the way her nose turned up ever so slightly. She stole my breath away because, deep down inside, I knew her. Was she really my Molly? Did she recognize me too?

"How was school, Nora?" Dr. Faye asked his daughter.

"Fun. I met a friend," Nora said, pointing at Clara. I stood up slowly, with caution. I was beginning to feel unwell.

"Are you alright, Becca? You look like you've seen a ghost."

I stared at the doctor as he held his blue-eyed daughter. She looked so much like him. There really was no explanation for what I had conjured in my head.

"I'm fine, doctor. Just a little light-headed is all," I said.

"I'm not your doctor anymore. Call me John."

"OK, John," I said, even more uncomfortable now that we were on a first-name basis.

"And do call me. We'll get these girls together," he said.

I blushed, "I will." I watched them walk away before I gathered myself. When Clara and I fastened our seatbelts, she began telling me about her day. A lot of it had to do with her friendship with Nora, and I may have pried just a little.

"So you two are friends?" I asked.

"Yeah!"

"That's so great! How did you know you were friends?"

"What?"

"Like how did you know you wanted to be her friend?" I adjusted my rear-view mirror so that I could see her face.

"Um, because, Mommy. I just know," she said, and like me, it was the only explanation that I could come up with too.

CHAPTER 23

Easton didn't get home from work until nearly midnight. He walked into our bedroom stealthily, trying hard not to wake me, but I hadn't been able to sleep. I watched his silhouette weave in and out of the bathroom, each time wearing one less layer. When he slipped in bed, I reached my hand on top of his chest and placed my head on his shoulder. I opened my mouth several times to tell him about Nora, but every time it ended in silence and shame. I knew that the hole in my heart had never healed from losing Molly. And I knew that this was my way of coping with that loss. I would have believed anything if it made her whole again. And there was the problem.

"What's wrong?" Easton asked when my tears dribbled to his shoulder. "Hey, what's wrong?" he sat up and wrapped his arms around me.

"It's Molly," I cried.

"Oh, honey. It's OK. Shhh. It's going to be OK," he said, rubbing my shoulder like he'd done a million times before.

"No. It's not that. Easton, I think she's alive," I said, sitting up.

"You what?" Easton shook his head.

"Clara met a friend today at school. She said she just *knew* that they were meant to be friends. She just knew!" I searched Easton's face lit by the moon for any inclination he might believe me. I saw no signs.

"Clara made a friend today?"

"Yeah, but she's not just a friend . . . She's her twin!"

"What? She looks just like Clara?" Easton's voice rose, and his back stiffened like a board.

"Well, no. Not just like her. I mean, actually, they don't look alike at all. But—" I stammered.

"I'm sorry, Beck. Help me understand right now, because I can't wrap my mind around this. You think Molly is alive because Clara made a friend?" Easton's tone was now sharp, and I could tell his patience was wearing thin.

"I know. I know I sound crazy. I'm not, though. There's something there. Something in the way she looked at me. Easton, you've got to believe me!" I cried. The desperation in my voice scared me. I didn't recognize myself. Easton sucked in a deep breath and hugged me tightly. I knew this wasn't what he wanted to come home to after a long shift, and it only made me feel more guilty for losing my wits. "I just miss her so much. I have this hole in my heart, Easton, and it won't heal. It never heals!" I sobbed, unsure of when it would ever end. If it ever could end. I cried until I was too exhausted to lift my head, and the tears had run dry. It reminded me of the nights I'd spent balling in my truck when Clara was a newborn. I hadn't cried like this for months, maybe a year.

"I'll tell you what. I'll do a little research when I have some time at work. Just get me some names, and I'll see what I can find," Easton said. I don't know if he said it because he was curious about Molly being tethered or if he said it to make me feel better, but either way, I'd sleep a little better knowing that this wasn't over yet. If my little girl was out there, I had to know about it.

"It's Dr. John Faye . . ." I whispered.

". . . Wait, wasn't that your doctor?" he asked. I looked up to him with all the strength I had left and watched him lose faith in me all over again. "You're not telling me you think he stole our baby . . . Are you?" Easton pulled away.

"I mean, I hadn't thought about it like that but . . . now that you say it . . ." My head spun with the possibilities.

"No. Beck No. I'm sorry. That's just not—"

"I know. I know. I just thought that maybe she became tethered, but now that you say it, he *was* there. Maybe he just stole her." I had been on drugs after all.

"Do you really think he would steal our baby and then move to our neighborhood?" Easton asked.

I thought about it. It would be pretty reckless, and he was a smart guy. "Yeah, you're right. He wouldn't do that."

"Beck, do you think you need to talk to someone?" Easton asked gently.

"Look, there's nothing a therapist is going to tell me I don't already know. So, no. I don't need to talk to anyone. I'll let you go to sleep, but just promise me you will look into Dr. Faye," I said.

"You really want me to look into your doctor?"

"Yes."

"Then promise me something in return. You won't do anything stupid."

"What? What would I possibly—" I started.

"Breaking into somebody's house. Does that sound familiar?" Easton crossed his arms over his chest.

I lifted my hands into the air and glared at the ceiling, remembering that Easton had been my partner in crime once upon a time. Now, he was a cop. "Yeah, I promise. I will not do anything stupid!"

My alarm didn't have to wake me in the morning. My eyes had still been strapped to the ceiling by the time it went off. I startled, turning it off quickly so that it wouldn't wake Easton. I'd been so ashamed of my late-night conspiracy theory that I hadn't been able to fall asleep. I tried to tell myself it was ridiculous, but when I dropped Clara off at school, and Nora looked at me, my hair stood on end. It took everything in me not to take her in my arms and squeeze her tight. Thank god I didn't. I'd probably have been taken away. As my luck would have it, Easton would be the one to cuff me. I pinched the bridge of my nose and inhaled slow and methodically.

I'd felt hopeless before when Molly passed, but this was a whole new kind of hopelessness. I hoped Nora was Molly. I hoped she was OK. I hoped I wasn't . . . insane. It felt that way sometimes, and now more than ever. I wished that Easton and Clara wouldn't see it. Though that crazy part of me was stronger than I wanted it to be, I'd do what I could to keep it hidden. I didn't believe it was the best side of me.

I sat in my empty house, growing more and more leery of Dr. Faye as the silence ticked by. I cleaned the house from top to bottom and had ventured into an old linen closet just to keep my body moving. It didn't help my mind from wandering, though, and most of my thoughts revolved around what I could do to ensure that both of my daughters grew up in a happy and healthy home. I thought of the future and wondered how I could finagle my way into the girl's life and not be cast aside if she were to move again.

A lawsuit was the only thing I could think of . . . Apart from kidnapping, but that went against my simple rule of not letting my family see just how crazy I'd become. Whatever I did, I couldn't jeopardize my life with Clara and Easton to chase after a life with Molly that may or may not exist. I'd already done that in the first six weeks of Clara's birth. It wasn't fair to any of them, Molly included. And though it was hard to look at Clara and not be reminded of what I'd lost in Molly, I learned to do it over time. I felt terrible that it was an instinct of mine, but there was no right or wrong with mourning the loss of your child. It all had to unfold in its own unique way. I was just grateful that my way ended with Molly coming back to me.

* * *

Concealing the battle within me was more difficult than I expected it to be. The best way I knew how was distance. I put as much distance between the Faye family and me as I could. It had been nearly four months since I laid eyes on Nora, and since then, my mental state had declined considerably. Easton and I would argue every time I brought it up, and eventually, I stopped talking about it. But every day at school pick up, I watched from the parking lot. John picked up most days, but on the days he didn't, a nanny would. They were on their second nanny, and I wondered what happened to the first. I hated seeing my daughter go home with a stranger. It had been isolating to watch from afar, and I wasn't sure I could do it any longer. Before today, I had barely been able to hold myself back. I knew my patience was wearing thin.

I bit my lip when Clara and Nora surfaced from their classroom, holding hands. It took a lot of willpower to hold myself back from asking Dr. John Faye for a play date. That's why I stood just outside my truck door when the doctor was under the overhang of the school. Originally, I was trying to wait for Easton to get back to me with his police research, but he never did. I waved when John glanced in my direction, then continued to bite a hole into my lip until the copper taste of blood had surfaced. I shook my head, trying to dispel the crazy, but I knew now it wasn't possible. All I ever wanted after having children was to protect them, and that was instinct. Instinct wasn't a habit that could be changed. I knew from experience. As much as I hated this obsessive, burning side of me, I had to learn to live with it.

Maybe it was the taste of blood in my mouth, or simply that my willpower had finally worn out, but before I knew it, something in me snapped. My legs were moving across the parking lot towards the overhang. My mind a battlefield, my legs taking long forward strides.

"Hi John, how are you?" I asked, coming up by his side.

He turned to me and smiled. "I'm well. How are you doing?"

"Great, hey, I was going to take Clara to the park after school today. Did you two want to join us?" *Don't Beck...*

"Um . . . Sure, I think we have time for the park," John said, reluctantly.

"Great! Oh, but it's kind of cold outside today. Should we just go to my house instead?" *Stop this Beck. . .*

"Umm . . . OK. That would work too."

"Yeah, because I have hot chocolate for the kids, so. . ." I nodded.

"Right," John shrugged, peering at me oddly. Did he think I was coming on to him? Was he into it? My eyes darted about and landed on my daughter.

"Hi, honey. Nora is going to come over for a play date today. Won't that be fun?" I asked, kneeling beside her and taking her backpack.

"Really?" She squealed. They both did. I stood, tossing her bag over my shoulder and smiling at the doctor.

"Follow me?" I asked. He nodded, looking somewhat unsure. I checked my watch. Easton would be home in the next hour, and I wondered if this fell under the 'doing something stupid' category or not. The thought dissipated when I realized I did not have hot chocolate at the house. How was I supposed to be luring this man and his daughter to our house when I didn't even have hot chocolate for the kids?

John pulled into our driveway after me, and when I opened the door, the girls ran down the hall towards

Clara's room leaving John and me alone. My face flushed at the awkwardness of it all, and as a result, my mouth ran a mile a minute, trying to fill the silence.

"Come on in. Can I get you some tea? Soda? Water? Um, I don't think I have hot chocolate, now that I think about it, but I'm sure I have some of the fun-sized chocolate bars leftover from Halloween if—"

"No, thank you."

"Oh. OK," I stopped rambling off the contents within our pantry to the man I thought may have stolen my child and closed the cabinet doors. I swallowed the lump in my throat and walked over to the sofa. Sitting across from him, I had to ask myself why he appeared so comfortable. Had he known that I knew? Was he going to steal Clara too? "So tell me about . . . Um. . ." The words caught in my throat as the girls came barreling down the hall, giggling.

"Man, I don't think I've ever seen Nora this happy," John said. I smiled, my eyes lingering on his before looking to the girls. Maybe this wasn't a reckless idea after all. The girls were having fun. Nora squealed and clapped her hands right in front of Clara's face, causing Clara to jump back. Both girls peeked into Nora's hands as she opened them ever so slowly. When her palms were open wide, they both giggled . . . identically. It was music to my ears. Did every little girl have a similar laugh? I didn't think so.

"What are you girls doing?" John asked.

"We're catching lights!" Nora said. My smile melted, leaving me with a low-hanging jaw. Then *smack!* Another clap. This one caught with a skip and a jump. I watched the girls peek inside Nora's hands with renewed hope and scream with delight when nothing had been there. I closed my mouth, but I couldn't stop my eyes from watering. Had this simply been how little girls played? Or had Nora been catching the love she saw surrounding her sister?

The front door opened, and Easton walked in. He stalled taking in the doctor on our sofa, and I used the distraction to blot my eyes. I stood up with trembling hands and motioned to Easton. "You remember Easton, my husband," I said.

Easton placed his hand on his gun, giving John a subtle warning that did not go unnoticed by either of us.

CHAPTER 24

"Easton, so good to see you again." John held his hand out, and I turned away from both of them to pull myself together. Easton had been such a loving and supportive man that I feared the reason he felt the need to warn the doctor with his subtle gesture. Easton was no longer the tall thin guy I had fallen in love with, he had packed on the muscle for his training, and his frame was quite impressive. When he was in uniform, his bullet-proof vest added to his bulk, making him quite intimidating. Why he needed to grip his gun in his own home was beyond me. Had it been because John was so good-looking? Easton had never been jealous before. Or was it something deeper than that? Had he discovered something about him? Something incriminating?

"Doctor," Easton said, taking his hand. The tension was so thick it could be cut with a knife. I sat back down, rubbing the back of my neck and looking anywhere but either of them. I could feel Easton's eyes burrowing into mine, and I knew he was cursing me for taking it a step too far. I didn't blame him. "So, I hear the girls have become fast friends," Easton said, breaking the ice. I took a deep breath, thankful for his presence.

"Yes, I was just telling Becca that I'd never seen Nora take to anyone quite like she has your daughter. It's refreshing to see."

"Is that so?"

"Yeah, it's been such a blessing, really. . ." John said.

"That's great. And you just moved here?" Easton asked as the girls ran down the hall, a trail of fireflies following them.

"This is Nora," I said. Easton looked toward the little girl, and I thought I saw it behind his eyes . . . The recognition. But it was my own emotions that hindered me from reading his face clearly. He watched her carefully, his eyes more than curious.

"Yes, we were closer to the hospital for work, but the schools out there—" John's voice echoed in the background as I watched Easton's eyes on Nora. It was then that I realized something . . . My eyes traveled from him to her. Nora didn't have dark hair and blue eyes like her father. Instead, she had them like Easton. She was nearly his spitting image, whereas Clara had looked just like me.

John continued to talk as Easton turned his attention to me. His eyes were filled with emotion, and I knew he'd seen what I had. I popped to my feet, breaking our gaze, and padded to the restroom before I lost it in front of John. I closed the door, locking it tight before pushing my back up against it. I sucked in several shattered breaths, none of which filled my lungs. I turned to the sink, gripping the cool porcelain top, and closed my eyes. *I was not crazy.* I was *not* crazy. When I opened my eyes and I saw my reflection staring back at me in the mirror, I was no longer a mother with a gaping hole in her heart. I was a mother with hope. I nearly didn't recognize myself.

I knew I couldn't hide in the bathroom forever, and it was a cowardly move in the first place to leave Easton out there alone. He'd probably been going through the same thing that I had been, but he was out there on the sofa having to act his way through it. I felt bad for him and all the acting that he had done in his lifetimes. I went to rescue him, but not before splashing cold water on my face.

"Hey, are you OK? It looks like you've got something up with your eyes?" John asked the second I sat back down.

"Oh, yeah. I'm allergic," I said.

"To what?"

"Cats," I said.

"Dogs—" Easton said.

"Oh?" John looked between us.

"Well, it's fur, really. I'm allergic to fur."

"That's too bad. It's probably me. We have a big cat at home. He's got the long fur and everything."

I snapped my fingers. "That's got to be it," I nodded.

"Well, I should get going. I don't want to make you sick," John said.

"Oh no, you just got here. . ." I checked my watch again. "Hey, I don't know if you guys are busy next Sunday, but it's Clara's sixth birthday, and we were going to throw her a little party. If you guys could make it?"

"Next Sunday?" John asked.

"Yes, just a small party. A couple of friends and the neighbors," I shrugged.

"That's so weird. That's Nora's birthday too."

There it was, the proof I didn't need. I tried to speak but couldn't. "A. Um—" I stammered.

"All the more reason to celebrate," Easton said, opening the front door with a stoic face.

"Yeah, you're right! Let me just talk to my wife and make sure she doesn't have any plans, and I'll get back to you," John smiled before calling for his daughter. *Our* daughter. Easton, Clara and I stared as the two of them walked down our driveway with sad eyes and heavy hearts. Watching her go was hard on all of us. Easton closed the door but didn't say anything. He only stood motionless with his head hung.

"Mommy, Nora says that we all have glowy lights," Clara said, raising her hands in the air.

"She does? *All* of us?" I asked.

"Yes. All of us," she said. My heart skipped a beat, causing me to cough. "What's the matter, Mommy?"

"Nothing, baby. I'm just so happy you made such a good friend." I kneeled in front of her and tucked her blond hair behind her ear. "Um, so do you see these glowy lights, too?" I asked.

"No. I can't see them. But she says they're there. She says she's going to catch one and give it to me." My chest tightened. I didn't know what it meant, but judging by the feeling it left behind, it wasn't a good thing. I turned and looked up at Easton to see the same grave look on his face that I felt in my heart. "Why are you sad, Mommy?"

I turned my attention back to Clara. "Well, baby, she's a good friend for trying. Those little glowy buggers can be hard to catch sometimes," I said, thinking back to the time that I tried to catch one myself. They were as real as the breath in my lungs, but when I grasped at them, my hand only passed through a pocket of warm air.

"I'm hungry," Clara said, snapping me back to the present. I stood up and passed by Easton to get Clara a snack, but not before I snuck a quick glance at him. His face was pale and somber. Eyes transfixed, distant. I didn't know what it all meant, but there was something in his demeanor that told me he did.

Dinner passed incredibly slowly as the conversations we needed to have hung just out of reach. I was bursting inside with every emotion. So much so that I couldn't pick the most prevalent one. My mind was running a marathon while my heart was sputtering. Clara talked about her new best friend —her only friend—while Easton and I stole glances at each other over the roasted chicken. Neither one of us had much of an appetite, and most of dinner had to be packed up as leftovers. By the time Clara went to sleep, and we finally had our chance to talk, neither one of us could find the words.

I sat on the sofa with a lap blanket pulled up to my chin while Easton made a wood-burning fire in the fireplace. Once the fire ignited, he sat next to me, and I draped his lap with half the blanket. A minute of heaviness passed between us before my head found his shoulder. The flames grew taller and wider, crackling and popping. My eyes glued to the white-hot flames. I still didn't know how to feel about the recent news, but at least I wasn't alone. I knew I could get through anything with Easton by my side. I had before. Surely, we would get through this, too.

"You know, I thought I was losing it? I thought I was actually going crazy. I felt myself slipping away . . . and this . . . monster . . . taking over me. It was a monster," I trailed off.

"You could never be a monster, Beck," Easton reassured me.

"I wanted to steal that little girl and run away with her," I said.

"Oh." Easton looked down at me, and I lifted my head off his shoulder to meet his gaze. "Really?" he asked.

"Well, I wasn't going to do it!" I said defensively. "For better or worse. You married me, for better or worse, just in incase you needed a reminder . . ." I said. I raked my hands through my hair. "I don't know. . .I just felt so helpless. And all I wanted to do was protect her as a mother should. It's my only job, and I failed."

"You didn't fail. You're an amazing mother. You've done everything you could—"

"But I lost her. I lost Molly." It was the absolute truth.

"Beck, I didn't want to tell you, but I did some background searches some time ago. Some of it was illegal, and some of it was—most of it was—on social media . . ." I straightened my back attentively. In all my crazy moments, I'd thought of kidnapping, breaking an entry, stalking . . . But I'd never thought of looking up the doctor's social media profiles. It should have been alarming to me, but I moved past it effortlessly. I never claimed to be a saint.

"And?" I asked.

"And, it looks like they adopted Nora when she was around six weeks old."

"They adopted her?"

"Yes."

"So, it *is* . . . Molly. . ."

"I can't say for sure. But—"

"But you know, don't you? You know deep down inside, that little girl is our Molly, don't you?" My voice was broken with the pain. It was in six weeks that I finally turned the corner on my depression. It wasn't because we had a memorial and I said goodbye to Molly; it had been because Molly was no longer alone. Someone adopted her and showed her the love she had deserved all along. That someone should have been me. Easton's eyes locked onto mine as he held in what he really wanted to say. He wasn't fooling anybody. I saw the way he looked at her.

"You know, she has your eyes. . ." I said.

And that's when Easton broke. He held his head in the palms of his hands. Elbows digging into his knees, his back began to quake. I didn't intend to hurt him, and the sight of him crumbling before me wasn't easy to witness. But I knew it was the sight of his confession. He didn't have to say he knew it was Molly because his body was screaming it from the inside out. We both knew it.

I rubbed Easton's back as mindless tears ran down my cheeks. I watched the fire dance till it no longer raged. Then, when Easton had no more left to give, he laid on the sofa and pulled me close to him. My back pushed to his chest and his arm wrapped around me tightly. I traced my finger over his skin mindlessly as I wondered if my life was back on track to becoming untethered. Surely having Molly back would put me on the path of living a happy and fulfilled life. That was if I could find a way to stay in it. Because it was a tremendous threat that the doctor would move, or even something so simple as stop returning my calls. It was all so fragile, like a house of glass. I needed to watch my every move, become strategic. Calculated. Because this was one game I couldn't afford to lose.

After Easton fell asleep, my fingers trailed from the skin of his arm to the metal of my cell phone. I was afraid of what I might find on the internet. All the secrets that were hidden right there in plain sight this whole time. Finding the doctor was easy. Too easy. Within seconds I was browsing through private moments. A baby wrapped tight in a blanket, a close up of Nora that looked identical to Clara. It stole my breath away, yet somehow my thumb found the strength to continue scrolling.

Several pictures with groups of people, family reunions, medical awards—I skipped it all. I scrolled and scrolled until I chanced upon the close ups of my precious daughter. Nora laughing with the tongue of a dog licking the side of her face. Nora at a dance recital when she was so tiny, her pink tutu could have swallowed her whole. Nora blowing out the candles on her third birthday. That's where I stopped because I could no longer take the sight of everything I had missed and shouldn't have.

CHAPTER 25

The week passed by slowly in anticipation of the girls' birthday. Every day a challenge new in itself, but one day closer to spending our first milestone with Nora. It was the driving force that kept me moving through the week. I would need to make this memory the best one yet. The birthday party had to be perfect, and I had to make a good impression on Nora's mother. We had exchanged a few texts about the party throughout the week, and she seemed nice enough, but if she didn't absolutely love me, it would destroy my chances of watching Nora grow up.

The doorbell rang, causing me to sweat through my second blouse even though it was the dead of winter. I opened the door, relieved to see it was only the neighbors. "Hi, Jackson! So nice to see you!" I said, waving the family inside.

I was changing my top for the third time when the doorbell chimed again. I took off running down the hall and ripped the door open—Brooklyn. "Oh, thank god you're here. I'm freaking out. I can't do this," I said, fanning myself in the doorway.

"Hey, hey, it's OK. You're going to be great. They're going to love you."

"You don't understand. They invited their parents too. I have many people I need to impress. And what happens if they recognize the similarities between Nora and Clara?" I asked.

"Come on," Brooklyn said, taking my hand and leading me back down the hall.

"Where are we going?"

"You can't meet them with sweaty armpits, and we can't have this conversation here in the doorway, either," Brooklyn said. I lifted my arm again and huffed at the sight of my underarms. I really had to pull myself together. Brooklyn closed the bedroom door behind me, and I ran my hands through my hair. "Look, remember what I told you? It's all going to be alright. You have to calm down," she said.

"But how do you know Brooklyn? How do you know?" I searched her eyes, looking for a sign that she knew something I hadn't. She sighed, then turned away from me to dig through my closet. "Brooklyn? Did you have a dream that you're not telling me about?"

"This one. Put this one on," she said, holding up a sun-kissed yellow top.

"Not that one, because yellow is cheery, and I don't want to appear too bouncy or energetic because what if she's an introvert and I just—"

"Put it on!" Brooklyn barked, causing me to jump. I did as she said. I would self-detonate if I didn't have her in times of weakness.

Brooklyn tweaked the buttons, and I asked again. "Did you have a dream?"

"I—" The doorbell rang, and I sucked in a breath. "Forget it. Let Easton handle it," she said. My eyes flickered from my closed bedroom door back to Brooklyn. "I . . . I haven't had a dream, but I know everything will be fine. Who wouldn't love you? Just go out there and be yourself." It was the worst advice. If only she had known just how unstable I had grown to be over the last several months.

I could hear the guests arriving, and I instantly regretted inviting the entire kindergarten class. I did so hastily when I thought the doctor was hesitant about my eagerness to have them over. I figured he couldn't say no if the entire class was coming. It turns out, I was right. He accepted the invitation for the shared birthday party when I announced to the class that invitations would be passed out after school. I had to run home and print off twenty invites that day. High-pitched squeals sounded through the walls, and I assumed Nora and her family had arrived.

"But what if they see through me? What if they can tell that something is off? We're not exactly the family next door," I said, rubbing out the worry across my forehead.

"And I'm not the girl next door, but I do a pretty damn good job of covering that up, don't I?" Brooklyn asked, placing her hands on my shoulders.

"That's because you 're a witch," I joked.

"I'm no such thing." Brooklyn smiled.

"Easton's an actor. He's been doing it forever. It's normal to you guys."

"Becca, Clara is six. You have been doing this for the past eight years now. You have got this. Nobody is going to think a thing about you or the girls. Honestly."

I took a minute to relax. Fill my lungs with one last breath before stepping into the interview of a lifetime. "I'm scared, Brooklyn. I don't want to lose my chance," I said.

"Honey, what's waiting for you out there is not a loss by any means," Brooklyn said, and for the first time, I believed it. I believed that life happened this way for a reason. I couldn't possibly know what that reason was, but I had to believe that I could make the best of it. I smiled and nodded. I started to walk out of the bedroom and into the rest of my life when, "Wait! That yellow is all wrong!" Brooklyn said.

When Brooklyn and I finally emerged from my bedroom, I wore a sky blue sweater and jeans. The house was filled with kids and parents alike. I waded through the crowd, handing out pleasantries and getting caught up in warm hugs. The small talk was encapsulating, and I excused myself several times as I looked for John and his family. I spotted Easton and made my way to him. His eyes looked me up and down, and a grin set in. "You, look—"

"Are they here? Have you seen them?" I asked, my eyes searching the crowd.

"Um, no. But your mother is," Easton's brows rose.

"My mom?" I asked. Last I heard, she would not make the party and living so far away it was completely understandable. Easton tipped his head in her direction, and I followed his line of sight to where my mom stood talking to Clara. I passed by Easton. "Mom?"

She turned to me and smiled pleasantly enough. "Becca! You look marvelous."

"What are you doing here?"

"Well, that's not a warm welcome," she stated dryly.

"I'm sorry. Hi. Hello." I hugged my mom, and Clara took off running when she saw new friends show up. So far, none of them had been Nora. "I just didn't think you were coming," I said.

"I know, but then I got thinking. This weekend was probably better than next month anyhow. Plus, I couldn't miss my only grandchild's sixth birthday party! What kind of grandmother would I be if I did that!" *Only grandchild.* The words rang through my mind, swirling till I felt dizzy. "I see your father didn't come. . ." My mom said. I didn't know what she had against the man. As far as I knew, she was the one who sabotaged their relationship. I shook my head, dispelling the unnecessary stress, and spotted Tanner making his way to the backyard dressed in uniform.

"Excuse me, Mom. I've got to say hello to my brother-in-law," I said, squeezing her shoulder as I left her side. As I approached Tanner, I saw Brooklyn intercept. I hadn't seen them together since the day they ended their relationship. I knew they had spoken, I just hadn't seen it myself, and it was nice to see them together. Tanner was smiling, and it actually looked genuine. I looked down at my watch, which revealed that John and his family were now nearly an hour late. My heart sank, thinking they might not show. I checked my phone to see if they had left any messages when Clara stopped me and asked if we could do the piñata. I sighed, looking around at all the kids. They were growing restless. Regardless of whether the Faye's showed up, I had an obligation to throw one heck of a birthday party.

"If everyone would like to grab a bag over here, and write their name on it, then we can line up and take turns at the piñata!" I called out. The kids ran to the bags, and I fought against the crowd to get to my cell phone. When I did, I had several messages unseen, but only one that I cared about. John had a delivery and would show up late if they could make it at all. Disappointment washed over me, but I still had a sliver of hope that they would come before the party was over. Either way, the show must go on. I owed it to Clara. And for the moment, she hadn't noticed that her sister wasn't here. *Sister.* I hadn't allowed myself to say that word until now, and it made my stomach flip.

I turned on the outside speakers and pushed through some party music. The kids jumped and danced in anticipation for their turn at the piñata. Easton yanked the rope, sending the candy stuffed unicorn soaring through the air. Clara spun, missing her strike, and we all cheered her on. She smacked it when Easton let her, and the crowd of parents clapped. The grin on my face, once wide, shrank when I scanned the yard again. It's an odd thing that happens when you're surrounded by people, yet still feel alone.

The party continued, and I threw myself into hostess mode. There was only an hour left before everyone would head out. Even so, my Molly had not yet arrived. Presents and cake had yet to pass, but I couldn't wait any longer. I sat Clara down in front of her gifts, and she shredded them. I set aside the gifts labeled Nora and the ones that were addressed to both girls. The pile of untouchable gifts grew with the times I checked my watch. Clara screamed over the dolls and stuffed animals while tossing the clothing behind her back. My cheeks burned as I reminded her repeatedly to be kind and thankful. When I looked out into the sea of parents, it was clear that none of them had expectations of graciousness at this age, and many of them laughed it off and nodded, saying their children were the same way.

When Clara's chubby cheeks dimpled, I lost my stomach. The air had turned brisk, and a chill settled down my back. Her sister had arrived; I was sure of it. The loud chatter quieted until I heard nothing at all. Time slowed frame by frame as beautiful Nora swept through the crowd leaving a trail of glowing lights behind her. My heart soared seeing her wide smile as her eyes fell upon Clara and the gifts. Soft tresses of dark hair curled around her face and sprawled over her shoulders.

I watched her in slow motion pull from her mom's hand and dash towards Clara. The sea of kids and parents parted, letting the second birthday girl through. And as the parents took a step back, my eyes stretched from the hand that was left behind. It was when I saw the doctor's wife—the woman dressed in scrubs with blue eyes and dark blond hair—that time had frozen completely. Just for a moment. My heart fluttered . . . faltering. Because I had never foreseen that the mother of my child would be Lindsay.

My best friend, Lindsay, from my first life. The one I hid my cancer from. The one I loved so deeply that I was afraid to let her down with my diagnosis. The one I hadn't seen in twenty-nine years. The mother of my child.

Time resumed, and the noise became deafening. I whipped my head away and ducked through the crowd. I ran from Lindsay. I raced into the house, heading for the confines of my bedroom, when John intercepted me along the way.

"Becca! I'm so sorry we're late. I had a delivery mid-morning," John said, giving me a quick handshake. I looked down at our hands, barely able to discern what he was saying. "Oh, and this is my mother, Mary, and my wife's parents are coming, they're just a little slow," John said, motioning down our driveway. I shook Mary's hand as my eyes stretched to see Lindsay's parents pushing their walkers towards us.

"Nice to meet you. Um, make yourself at home. Everyone is out back. . ." I said as I backed up slowly before turning on my heels and running down the hall. When I reached my bedroom, I slammed the door closed and pushed my back up against it, breathing heavily. The door pushed open, and I lurched forward. Easton and I collided in a spell of panic.

"Where's my hat?" he said, breathless. His eyes scanning the bedroom before landing on mine. I didn't know where his disguise was, and in the moment, I couldn't comprehend much more than the sound of my heart gushing in my ears. But one thing was resoundingly clear—this was the path that would set me free.

THANK YOU

Thank you for reading The Kindred Soul of Nora Faye. Please take the time to leave a quick review or rating. It would mean so much to me!

Thanks for the support,
Laura C. Reden

ABOUT THE AUTHOR

* * *

Laura C. Reden is an emerging author who likes to add paranormal and fantasy twists while tugging at the heart strings.

Overcoming the struggles of dyslexia, Laura found that creative passion and hard work triumphs over her disadvantage.

Laura is a Southern Californian native, wife, and mother of two daughters. Her pastimes include video production, pottery, and horseback riding. While she received an education in social and behavioral science, she currently works as the chief financial officer for her family-owned law firm in San Diego.

If you are interested in staying updated on new releases, subscribe to my monthly email list. It's short and sweet with opportunities to help name characters, get advanced review copies, and even have your pet featured in upcoming scenes.

https://www.subscribepage.com/redenbooks

Xoxo,

Laura

bookbub.com/authors/laura-c-reden
instagram.com/author.laurac.reden
facebook.com/lauracreden

LAURA C. REDEN

DREAMS ARE FICKLE, EMOTIONS ARE BOLD.

THE
PHANTOM SERIES

CAUGHT BETWEEN WORLDS,
KINSLEY WILDE CAN SEE THE DEAD,
MANIFEST HER DREAMS, AND CONJURE HER FEARS.

BOOK CLUB NOTES: